Praise for ~

"*Belonging* is an endearing
encountering the generosity
fulness through circumstances in her life. You will be
encouraged as she deals with her difficult past. Ms. Owen
presents the characters in a way that they shine. You will
enjoy knowing them, and will want to know more about
them. This story shows God's faithfulness, and the verses
were a reminder of God's desire to love me and guide me
in His Way."

Coralyn Bunn
Pastor's Wife

"A suspenseful tale of young love, where the grace of
God triumphs against the odds."

Debra Stoeber
Ladies' Bible Teacher

Belonging

Belonging

Luellan Owen

Tate Publishing & *Enterprises*

Published by Tate Publishing & Enterprises, LLC
127 E. Trade Center Terrace | Mustang, Oklahoma 73064 USA
1.888.361.9473 | www.tatepublishing.com

Tate Publishing is committed to excellence in the publishing industry. The company reflects the philosophy established by the founders, based on Psalm 68:11,
"The Lord gave the word and great was the company of those who published it."

Book design copyright © 2008 by Tate Publishing, LLC. All rights reserved.
Cover design by Stephanie Woloszyn
Interior design by Isaiah R. McKee

Published in the United States of America

ISBN: 978-1-60462-992-7
1.Christian Fiction: General Romance   2. Christian Fiction: Suspense

08.06.23

Dedication

In memory of my husband, Clay Owen,
who always believed in my writing.

$\mathcal{A}$cknowledgements

My sincerest appreciation goes to my editor, Jennifer Scott, at Tate Publishing, for her patience as I struggled with a new computer in the back and forth editing process. Thanks is due also for her encouragement and her desire to meet my communication needs. Also my thanks go to Stacy Baker, Jesika Lay, Dave Dolphin, Stephanie Woloszyn, and the production staff at Tate Publishing for making *Belonging* a reality.

I want also to express my gratitude for the encouragement of Pat Breisch who believed in me. Also the ladies of The Lunch Bunch, especially Jackie Ward and Marjorie Orr, who gave me confidence. And for the exuberance of the Ladies Bible Study at church, when they learned of my endeavor. Also thank you to my grown children, Mark, Lynn, Eric, and Gregg who, being careful for their mom, stood by me with patience.

*I*ntroduction

As a young, married woman, I spent vacation time in the mountains of Colorado at Spring Canyon, a conference center of the Officer's Christian Fellowship. The love I've had for that place, the fragrance of Christ and the beauty of His creation, was the seed that encouraged *Belonging*. On one excursion we visited the ghost town of St. Elmo. Years later, a young friend in St. Louis bought mountain property and hired a builder who became smitten with her. This began the plotting. It is my prayer that you might smell the pines as you read *Belonging,* and it might encourage you with the fragrance of Christ.

"Teach us to number our days aright, that we may gain a heart of wisdom," (Psalm 90:12).

One

Diana Laramore didn't much care for Jonathan Somes. His eyes were always guarded behind thick glasses, and he only said what was necessary, never friendly. So why had he insisted that she come to St. Elmo from her Denver office? Anxiety covered Diana like a rash. Sutton's lawyer had a lot of power. She had installed a computer system at Sutton three years ago. Had something gone wrong? Why had he insisted she come now?

Somes, standing behind his mahogany desk, removed his spectacles.

"Miss Laramore," he said, gesturing toward a chair. "Thank you for coming. I won't take up a lot of your time, so I'll get right to the point." He sat down and adjusted his bifocals. "William F. Sutton left a piece of land to you in his will." He looked at her, his brows arching over the rim of his glasses. This was a surprise.

"Left me some land? I read about his passing, but I never expected…" She leaned forward.

"I know." Mr. Somes smiled. "W. F. was eccentric and unpredictable. But there are some stipulations." He paused, shuffled papers, and continued. "The land is made up of one hundred and twenty-five acres of forest, bordering Sutton on the north and the national forest on the west. You'll have to agree to conservation and tree harvesting that has always been done." He paused then, watching her stunned reaction. "Are you all right, Miss Laramore?"

"Yes, I think so," she said.

"W. F. also arranged for a trust fund to be used for land improvement. Mainly, you must put a livable building on the land and occupy it before winter sets in, or it reverts back to Sutton. If you fulfill that requirement and the land becomes yours by title, you must agree to always keep it whole and to sell its harvested trees to Sutton Industries." Somes handed her the papers. "If you agree, please sign here. As you can see, this will require nothing financial on your part. The trust fund is designed to provide the money for construction and upkeep." Diana examined the papers through unbelieving eyes.

Raising her head she questioned, "I can't believe it's that simple. There's got to be a catch somewhere?" She said, "You mean all I have to do is sign?"

"That's all. If you decide you don't want the land, then just let the time go by without doing anything." He leaned back in his chair and clasped his hands behind his head. Smiling, he said, "W. F. told me he was most impressed by your abilities and your dedication to your work. I think he felt you needed a place to escape to, to recharge, so to speak." He sighed and leaned forward. "In effect, Sutton Industries will still reap the benefits of the land, but so will you."

Diana smiled, remembering William F. Sutton was much like a grandfather. She was always comfortable with him and eventually told him about a dream she had to find a retreat where she could go when she was between projects. He said, "The Lord will guide you, my dear. Delight yourself in Him, and He will bring it to pass." He invited her to dinner with his wife, and through all that, they led her to faith in Christ.

"I'll sign it," she said. Diana left with the name and address of the company builder required by the will. Following a detailed map from Somes, she drove up through timbered country. The air was cool and crisp for the end of April. She passed islands of snow like quilt patches and turned off the road onto gravel at a "No Trespassing" sign. The road led to a meadow bordered by tall pines growing up the mountain slopes. She stopped and noticed that the road circled the meadow and then connected again. The peaceful beauty filled her with unexpected joy. *This must be God's will. W. F. was so close to the Lord. How could I not love this place?*

As she walked, the smell of the pines filled her. Climbing a bit, she found a rough outcrop of rock to sit on. Thinking over the events in Somes office and remembering W.F., and his passion for his company, his church, and his Lord, she knew she could not walk away from this challenge. *I can't believe this is just for me. This is a perfect spot for a building, a cabin, a hideaway, even a chalet.*

A drive could come up the incline. There's plenty of level space in back, and the view is…

A pickup truck moved into the meadow and pulled in behind her car. She watched a tall, muscular man with dark brown hair get out to scan the meadow. He wore a fleece-lined, denim jacket and blue jeans. He dug fishing gear out of the back and made his way down through the scrubby brush to the creek. *Is this place well known? Or, maybe he's from Sutton.* Diana didn't mind an occasional visitor, but if it was common knowledge for the town's fishermen—*come to think of it there was a "No Trespassing" sign.*

She got off her perch and walked down to where he was fixing his line.

"Hello. Do much fishing here?" she said.

He scowled with narrowed brows. "As often as I can." Then he continued with his fishing gear. She decided to ignore his manner.

"Do many people come up here?"

"No." He looked up at her through steel gray eyes, and she sensed anger in the hardness in his jaw. She shivered inside as he looked her up and down.

"You must live near here. Do you come here often?" she said, hoping he would offer more.

"Yeah." His jaw clenched and he returned to his pole and reel.

Awful man, she thought, and turned on her heel toward her car. *If he comes here to fish he might think he owns the place. I'll have to set him straight on that. What cheek he must have when the sign was very clear—"No Trespassing."*

I think I'll find out who he is. Diana decided that since she had some time between assignments, she would try to set up a meeting with that builder.

Jake McKibbon grinned behind the Carter Hotel desk. He was born in St. Elmo and remembered the early days. Everyone knew him for the fixture he was.

His blue eyes twinkled, "Well, I'll be! Diana Laramore! You back here for Sutton?" He leaned forward with a serious sadness, "You know W. F. is gone now."

"Yes, I know," she sighed. "I miss him."

"He and I were good friends, known him most of my life. He grew up around here too. They don't make them kind anymore. Fine man he was, a deacon in the church too."

"I found that out too," Diana said, smiling. "He led me to Christ."

"You don't say! I first met him in Sunday School. I was eight and he was nine. He had fine parents too. We used to go huntin' together. Then him and his wife started a Bible study, and Charlene and I went. Charlene's gone now, but those were rich days. God's been awful good to me."

"Me too, Jake. Is my old room available?"

"Sure is." He handed her the key.

Climbing the stairs, Diana mused about what Jake had said. *Sunday School, Bible study, a lifetime of knowing and living with the Lord. That must have been wonderful.* Her parents had given her everything. They had loved her and brought her up with proper values, but not in church. The year after she graduated from college, they took a trip to Mexico and were killed on a mountain road in an accident. Now with sadness, she remembered that awful time. *But Lord, you've made up for that. I have so much in other ways, and I thank you.*

Standing by the window, she deliberately pushed the pain away and noticed several people entering the library across the street. Deciding to find out how log cabins are built, she put her things away, glanced in the mirror, and let herself out.

Entering the old brick library, she crossed to the desk where a small plump woman with graying hair sat pouring through some files. Angie Carlson was the woman who became her friend three years ago. Diana looked at her lovingly.

"Hello, Angie. I thought I'd surprise you today." The older woman looked up and her face lit with a grin.

"Well, for goodness sake, Diana Laramore! I'm so glad to see you. I got your Christmas letter, but I didn't expect to see you face-to-face!" She came around the desk and the two friends hugged. She was a woman born in the area, married after college, and moved away to teach school. After nineteen years of marriage, her husband passed away. Never having children, she decided to move back to St. Elmo when the position of librarian became available. Now nearly ten years later, Angie was a happy, well-informed, and respected member of the community. "What brings you back here, more work for Sutton?"

"No, something even better. Can you go to lunch with me, and I'll tell you all about it?"

Angie made arrangements, and the two walked down

the street to the Hub, a small cafe where most of the town always gathered for lunch. Angie knew them all and greeted each one. A few remembered Diana. After ordering, Angie leaned across the table, "Okay, now tell me what's up!" Diana described her meeting with Somes and the terms of W. F.'s will. Angie smiled.

"That sounds like something he would do. Have you decided to go ahead?"

"I think so. I love this town. I found Christ here. Denver is so big and impersonal. You know I really have no family anymore. Since Mom and Dad died, and I left Houston, Denver became my home, such as it is, except I'm really not there much. Althea and I share an apartment. With her nursing and my work, sometimes the only communication we have is notes left on the blackboard. Coming up here is so appealing and the peace of that meadow… it would give me a place to escape to."

"Escape to? How about a home? This is a great place to live. The Christians here are so welcoming, and I would love to have you here permanently."

"Well, Denver would be a long commute, but certainly on weekends. That is unless I could persuade Worthington Associates to move up here." Diana rolled her eyes and laughed.

"Fat chance," Angie agreed. "So, what can I do?"

"Has your establishment got any information about building log cabins or any plans I could see?" After lunch they returned to the library and Angie found two books and a magazine with an article about "A" frames and mountain retreats.

"You can take these with you. I'll fix you a card. And when you get ready to line up a builder, I can give you some names."

"Oh, Somes gave me the name of a Mr. Cureau."

"Oh." Angie smiled like she knew a secret but didn't elaborate. "Happy reading, dear."

Later in the dining room, the hostess seated her by a heavily draped window. After ordering, she noticed the same man who was fishing earlier that day, only now he was dressed in a beige, suede, sport jacket and dark brown slacks with a nice tie. *Hmm,* she thought. *Certainly not the itinerant fisherman.*

He was polite, listening to the attractive redhead opposite of him. Diana decided he was a little bored because he glanced around the room as the woman talked. On one of those glances he saw Diana, and she stared at him. He obviously recognized her, but not before his companion sensed his interest and glanced toward Diana. Her pulse quickened. She was uncomfortable and resolved not to look his way again.

As she ate, she knew the two were discussing her. The woman nodded and glanced toward Diana, and the man gave short answers as the redhead did most of the talking. Wondering what they were saying about her, she finished her meal. She knew she would never see him again and soon dismissed her thoughts. She would contact that builder in the morning.

• • •

"May the favor of the Lord our God rest upon us; establish the work of our hands for us" (Psalm 90:17a).

Two

Diana opened her eyes and stretched. Glancing at the clock, she reached for her Bible and settled herself against the pillows.

> Blessed is the man who does not walk in the counsel of the wicked or stand in the way of sinners or sit in the seat of mockers. But his delight is in the law of the Lord, and on his law he meditates day and night. He is like a tree planted by streams of water, which yields its fruit in season and whose leaf does not wither. Whatever he does prospers.
>
> Psalm 1:1–3 (NIV)

Diana closed her Bible and placed it on the table beside the bed. *I want to be like that tree, Lord. Guide me this day.* Rising, she found the builder's number and dialed. The *hello* at the other end of the phone was commanding.

"Mr. Cureau, I'm Diana Laramore. Jonathan Somes gave me your name. I would like to meet with you about a building project. Could I make an appointment for sometime this morning?" she said.

"I have to come into the village today. I can meet you in an hour. Are you staying at the hotel?"

"Yes, I am. How will I know you?"

"Never mind, I'll find you." And he hung up.

He doesn't waste words. I hope he doesn't waste time as well. After reading about building last night, I assume it'll take all summer. Somes words were clear that Nicholas Cureau would be the builder since he's under Sutton's contract. She reckoned that Cureau expected her and knew what she wanted, since he was with Sutton.

After breakfast in the lobby, she chose a corner with a comfortable chair, because she could watch the entrance and be inconspicuous. Soon the same man she'd seen in the meadow and again in the dining room stepped inside. She watched him as he paused a bit and glanced around. He wore light gray slacks with a maroon sweater and a windbreaker. When he saw her he moved straight toward Diana. She didn't have time to think before he stood there.

"Miss Laramore, I'm Nick Cureau," he said.

"Hello... again." He pulled up a chair and folded into it.

"I wasn't very nice yesterday..."

"Your hospitality didn't overwhelm me." He continued, his jaw set in a hard line.

"I hope we can work together."

"Do I have a choice?"

"As I understand it, neither of us do. It might be good to call a truce for the time being," he said. She studied him for a long moment. He was well-built, handsome in fact, with a kind of boyish quality. It was true that they were in a situation that neither had planned. Thinking she might as well make the most of it, she smiled.

"Okay, truce. I assume you know why I called you since you know who I am."

"Yes," he nodded. "You need to put a building up there, and I'm supposed to get it done." He looked away toward the window. She sensed a sadness when his jaw tightened as he turned back to her. "So, do you have an idea of what you want up there?"

"Well, I know there has to be a fireplace, and a picture window looking out on the meadow. I'd like to have a couple of bedrooms and maybe a loft, though I don't know what I'd put up there, yet. It just seems that a mountain cabin needs a loft." She paused and felt silly. "I guess you can see I'm a greenhorn about these things."

"I've got some plans in my office. They've all been built for the company so they meet the standards. They might give you some ideas, or if you see something you'd like just as it is."

"Okay. When would be a good time?"

"How about now? I can drive us over there. Then we can go up to the meadow."

She was surprised by the plush interior of his pickup. As they drove along, she stole a glance at his profile, the firm jaw line, straight nose, high forehead, and wavy brown hair. Her first impression was that of an angry man.

Finally, they turned off down a winding, gravel road to a lovely, rustic home surrounded by tall pines. Old snow still covered the ground in protected areas. He unlocked a side entrance without comment. He seemed tense, his mouth was a hard line. His office was well ordered. A large drawing board with a drop light was next to a bin with numerous rolls of blueprints. Beyond there was a table with assorted drawing tools and next to that a bookcase nearly full of books. On another wall, a leather couch behind a wide coffee table was flanked by two architect's lights. On the counter under a big window, his computer, printer, and ham radio were arranged to be reached by the swivel chair at his desk.

He led her to the couch and went over to the bin. Selecting several blueprints, he unrolled one and said, "This one has about 1500 square feet with two bedrooms."

They bent over the plan. Diana asked several questions, and he answered them. Then he pointed to a number of renderings on the walls, indicating which one went with this plan. She looked at all he had selected, asking questions, and then went over to examine the paintings.

"These are beautiful. Did you do them?"

"Part of the job." She noticed a larger rendering, handsomely framed, aside from all the others.

"What about this one? Do you have the blueprints?"

"No." It was sharp and clipped and made her turn to

look at him. He frowned and stared at the plans on the table. His jaw was set.

"Did I say something I shouldn't have? I'm sorry." She returned to the rendering. It was lovely. She could see the structure was massive, much more than her five or so rooms. His expression was pained as she turned back to look at him.

"No," he said. "Not your fault. It's just that I had some plans once. " She had no words for that awkward moment. *Futures have a way of falling down in mid-flight. I remember…*

Putting away memories, Diana came back to the table and selected one of the plans.

"I really like this one. I like the way the bedrooms and bath are configured, and the fireplace has an outside wood pass-through. I like that. And there's an openness in the living area which means that I could be in the kitchen and still see out the big window."

"Okay." He was now relaxed. The scowl was gone. "Let's take a run over to the meadow." Nick put the extra plans away in the bin.

"Is it far from here?" she asked.

"It's just on the other side of that ridge." He indicated the crest of trees toward the back of his house. "Takes about fifteen minutes."

They drove along in silence and finally stopped in the clearing where she had been yesterday. She pointed toward the spot where she had perched.

"Could it be built over there?"

"Depends how deep that rock goes. There's a stretch

behind it that would require some clearing. It might take down about three trees. But that shouldn't be a problem. "They walked over to the area." You'll need a septic tank up here, and there's a spring that feeds the meadow. We can pump water from there into the house."

"Won't this all have to be surveyed?" she asked.

"No, that was done several years ago. I'll need to get some heavy equipment up here to clear the ground and get ready for the foundation." Then he unrolled the blueprints. "You said you wanted the window to face the meadow. That's good. You'll get the morning sun that way. And your living room would be about where we're standing, like this." He stretched the blueprint, and she grabbed the edge. "The window would face east and to the left would be north." He was calculating the sun as he stood looking toward the meadow. "You should eliminate windows on the north because of the cold, and turn the top floor to face south with openings onto a deck, since there would be space."

"Yes, I like that. A deck off the bedrooms," she said.

"I'll need to draw up the plans."

"When will that be done?"

"I could have it by the weekend."

"Could I see it next Saturday?"

"I think so, unless something comes up. Maybe I'd better have a number where I can reach you just in case." He rolled up the plans, and they walked towards the truck. "I'll drive you back to town and get that information. You should know where I can be reached too."

On the ride to the hotel, Nick was quiet, and she

sensed that he didn't want to talk. Diana watched the road and pictured her cabin, the big window facing the meadow, the two bedrooms opening onto a deck. She imagined the stone fireplace with a mantle, and maybe her grandmother's clock there. Mentally she placed rugs on the floor and curtains at the windows. She wouldn't have a telephone, at least not right away, but then her boss would probably demand it. *Oh well,* she thought. *I'll solve all that later.*

As they arrived at the hotel, he reached in the glove compartment for a pad and pencil. After exchanging phone numbers, she thanked him and climbed down from the truck.

Later up in her room she tried to figure him out. *He seems nice enough, but he's angry about something. I wonder… I didn't sense that he's a Christian. He's nice looking… organized, very talented. I wonder if his anger has anything to do with that large picture? When he said 'no'… Something must have happened in his past—even yesterday in the meadow…*

After lunch she packed up her things, putting the paper with Nick's phone number in her appointment book. Gathering up her things, she felt regret leaving St. Elmo. It had been a good weekend.

• • •

"Better is open rebuke than hidden love, Wounds from a friend can be trusted," (Proverbs 27:5, 6a).

Three

Arriving back at the apartment, an attractive, dark-haired girl was in the kitchen fixing her meal when Diana let herself in. Althea grinned.

"How'd it go? Are you hungry? I read your note Friday. What's going on?"

"Whoa, not so fast," Diana said as she dumped her bag. Osgood, Althea's gray, tiger cat, rubbed against her leg, his tail held high. Althea filled a second plate with spaghetti and brought it to the coffee table, her curiosity ill concealed.

"I'm dying, you've got to tell me." As the girls ate, Diana told her about Sutton's will, the meadow, and Nick Cureau. Althea leaned back into the sofa. "Amazing! It's wonderful. But you don't seem overjoyed."

"You know, I'm always looking for what God wants, and I just can't believe it's all for me. A wonderful place to relax in but that just benefits me. And gifts like this are hard for me to accept," Diana said.

"But Diana, you accepted the Lord's gift of salvation. Can't you believe this is from Him as well? He gives us all good things to enjoy."

"You're right. He must be teaching me about accepting things without earning them. That's something I've had a hard time with."

"Maybe the 'earning' part will come when the building starts. What's this Cureau like?" Althea said.

"Very good-looking."

"Really, tell me."

"There's nothing to tell. He's all business, and besides, I think he must be taken. I saw him with a redhead in the hotel last night. And I certainly don't need a relationship to complicate my life. I don't think he's a Christian."

"Speaking of relationships," Althea cut in, "Roger called. Wants you to call him."

"What did he want?"

"Didn't say."

"Well, I'll see him at work tomorrow. I don't really want to call him, I'm tired, and I really want to get a good night's sleep. Roger can wait."

The girls cleaned up the kitchen, and Althea got ready for her night duty. Diana unpacked, put on her pajamas, and read for awhile. She was propped up with pillows when Althea poked her head through the door and let Osgood inside.

"See you in the morning. I'll lock the door on my way out." The cat jumped up on the bed and settled himself beside Diana, who absently began to stroke him.

The next morning, Althea let herself in as Diana was

putting on the last of her makeup. "Looks like it might snow out there. Better go prepared."

"Rats! I can do without that!" Climbing into her coat, she let herself out. It smelled like snow, and the western sky was overcast. Driving to work, Diana thought of the week ahead and the pressing issues on her desk. She parked in the garage beside Roger as he was getting out of his car. He waved and waited to walk to the elevator with her.

"Did you get my message last night?"

"Yes, but it was so late. What did you need?"

"Rumor has it that you and I will be working on that proposal for the Foster Development Corporation."

"Really? I thought they weren't interested."

"They reconsidered, realized they'd outgrown their system, more cost effective over time to put in a new one."

"What makes you think we'll be doing the work?"

"Their rep called Bill Saturday, and he called me. It'll come up in the meeting this morning." They stepped off the elevator and entered the reception area.

"I'll see you later, Roger. We can talk about it then." She turned to Anne Kimball, the receptionist, collected her messages, and went into her office.

The meeting did assign Diana and Roger to the Foster project. Roger was a friend, and Diana wanted to keep it that way. She knew he would like to be more than a friend, and Diana suspected she would have to let him know her boundaries again.

Roger knocked on her door, "I told Bill that both of us

should fly up to Foster's on Wednesday. We could cut the survey time by half and be back here to write the proposal a lot sooner."

"What did he say?"

"It's up to you." He smiled in a suggestive way. She drummed her fingers on the desk top.

"I have to finish up things," looking straight into his face. "And I think you can do the survey just as well alone. Besides it will cost the company more money to fly us both." Roger was pensive a moment.

"Okay," he sighed. Then he rocked back on his heels and stuffed his hands in his pockets. "Would you have dinner with me tonight instead?" She smiled.

"Sure. Do you want to go from work or pick me up later?"

"Later. How's seven?"

"Good."

Althea was fixing her evening meal when Diana got to the apartment.

"Well, did you make contact with Roger?" she asked.

"Yes. He asked me to dinner tonight. We've been assigned the Foster project."

"Hmmm. Then maybe you two will get together. I really like Roger. I don't see how you can resist those blue eyes."

Roger Aymes does have nice eyes, Diana thought. Althea had known Roger for about a year and she'd mentioned his eyes before. He was fun to be with, reminding Diana of the fraternity men she dated in college. He was like Mark, who she'd fallen in love with and was engaged to marry their last year at school. Only Mark backed out the day of graduation to go home to marry the girl next door, the girl he'd been groomed for by wealthy parents who had his life all planned. The rejection still hurt, but since she'd become a Christian, she realized how weak Mark really was and knew it had been a good thing. Changing to a blue, silk dress with long sleeves, she brushed her blond hair and fixed her makeup.

Roger was on time. Althea, about to leave for work, answered the door. Diana heard them talking from her bedroom. Althea was laughing about something Roger said. *Althea likes him. I'm glad. I wish Roger would really get interested in her…*

Later in the restaurant, after ordering prime rib, Roger leaned toward Diana.

"So, tell me about your weekend. What happened with Sutton? Do they need some updating?"

"Actually it was personal, not connected with business."

"Personal? It's been a couple of years since you were up there, before I came on staff. What gives?"

"When I installed their system I met Mr. Sutton, the president. He has since passed away, and he left me a piece of land in his will."

"You're kidding!"

"There's a catch, though. I have to put a livable building on it or it reverts back to Sutton. There are some other things too."

"Are you going to do that?"

"Yes, I think so. The money is provided. I don't have

anything to lose, really. It's a lovely spot, perfect for a log cabin overlooking a meadow."

"You went there?" His eyes were wide with surprise.

He questioned and she answered, telling him about Nicholas and the plans he was devising.

"I'll probably need to go this next weekend. If the plans are set, Nick can get started. I really only have the summer, so I can't waste any time."

"Sounds like you may need some help. I'm available."

"Not this weekend. You'll be in Seattle."

"True."

As the waiter brought dinner, Roger ordered a bottle of Bordeaux from the wine steward. Everything seemed perfect: candlelight on the table, wine in her glass, an attractive man sitting across from her, music playing in the background, and a delicious meal before her. Roger was everything: intelligent, kind, and interested in her welfare. However, she felt nothing for him. They ate without speaking for a while then Roger reached for his wine.

"You know, Diana, I could make it back in Friday night, and we could go up to St. Elmo together Saturday morning."

"No, not this weekend." She was adamant. "There's not much to see, and besides, the storm has probably dumped snow up there." Inwardly she cringed. *You are the last person I want in tow this weekend...*

"You're probably right," he admitted. "I was just looking for an excuse to be with you. You know how I feel about you."

"I like you, Roger. You're a good friend," she cut in.

"That's not what I mean, and you know it." She smiled.

"Roger, we've had this conversation before. I care about you as a friend, but beyond that…"

"Okay. But I won't give up." There was a long silence between them. Finally the atmosphere warmed, and they discussed Foster and the needs there. When Roger took her home, he said, "I'd ask to come in, but tomorrow starts early." He took her key and unlocked her door.

"I had a good time, Roger. Thanks." Diana gave him a hug.

Roger flew off to Seattle on Wednesday, and Diana spent the rest of that week clearing up work that was pending. On Friday she called Nick. The plans were ready, and they agreed that she could see them the next day.

Some hours later, Angie called. Diana was surprised.

"How did you get my number?"

"I was going across the street for lunch and ran into Nick Cureau. I asked him if he had been in touch with you, that we'd had lunch last week. He gave me your number. How are things going?"

"Okay. I'm coming out to see the plans tomorrow."

"Well, that's kind of what I called about. I assume you'll be making the trip out here often. Why don't you consider using my guest room and save yourself some money? I'd love the company, and you could just come and go as you need to. In fact why don't you come out tonight after work and we'll get you settled in?"

"Oh, Angie, that's so nice of you. I would love it. I think I'll take you up on your offer." Diana looked at her watch. It was a little after four. "You know, there's nothing pressing here. If I leave now I could probably get away from the apartment by six, which would put me in St. Elmo around eight."

"Good! Don't bother with supper. I'll have a bite when you get here." Diana straightened her desk, picked up her purse, and told Anne where she'd be for the weekend. This was Althea's weekend off-duty, and Diana felt guilty that she wouldn't be there, or that she couldn't ask Althea to accompany her to St. Elmo.

The two girls talked while Diana packed her overnighter. Althea had a date with a friend at church. Snapping her case shut, Diana hugged Althea and put on her coat. Osgood was up on the bed, and she reached over to scratch him behind the ears.

"Osgood, you keep an eye on your mistress. Be a good watch kitty."

She got in her car and began the drive out of the city. Finally reaching the outskirts, she made good time, and by eight o'clock, Diana was driving up the gravel road to Angie's lovely, old home. Angie had the porch light on and heard Diana arrive. She came out on the step.

"I'm so glad you came tonight. Can I bring anything in?" she said. Diana grinned a greeting and gave Angie her cosmetic case. The two went inside to the warmth of a glowing fire. Angie's home had not changed much since Diana's time in St. Elmo. Family antiques kept company with calico in shades of rose and green. A lovely oriental rug graced her floor. Diana sniffed.

"Something smells wonderful. Can I help?" she said.

"No." Angie laughed. "Let me show you your room. By the time you wash up, I'll have dinner out."

She led Diana up the stairs to a room with a canopy bed spread with a fluffy pink comforter and pillows. An arm chair and lamp stood in one corner, a dresser nearby. A private bath offered up the fragrance of rose soaps.

Dinner was delicious, and they chattered throughout the meal. Diana told Angie about the cabin site and the plans and about meeting Nick.

"I'm wondering why I didn't meet him when I was here," she said.

"He came to St. Elmo just after you were here. Nick keeps to himself a lot. And I think he travels too. I'm not sure just what he does besides Sutton. But I know he has family money."

"When I went out to the sight for the first time, he showed up to fish, and he was downright nasty." Diana made a face.

"Nick was engaged to Mr. Sutton's niece, and last year she was killed in an airplane crash. I don't think he's ever gotten over it." Angie sighed. "The man all but went into hibernation. No one saw him for weeks, and when any-one did, he was not pleasant. People just left him alone after a while."

"Well, he's getting around now," Diana said. "He was with a redhead last Saturday night in the hotel dining room. He seemed to be enjoying himself, and I must say she was dressed to kill." Diana finished her coffee.

"That would be Carol McKenzie, Lloyd Arbuckle's secretary."

"Who's Lloyd Arbuckle?"

"He stepped into W. F.'s place in the company. Took over running it. He was on the board of directors in New York, and he brought Carol with him."

"What's he like?"

"Keeps pretty much to himself, I guess. Not like W. F. used to be. No one really knows too much about him. He moved here to take over the company." Angie began clearing the plates and Diana got up to help. The two quickly put away the food, straightened the kitchen, and settled on the sofa in front of the fire.

Diana stared into the fire, watching the flames.

Mesmerized, she said, "I remember lots of times in our living room in front of the fire when I was growing up. I used to do homework there, mom was usually stitching something, and dad would be reading the paper. I can get hypnotized watching the flames. You have such a pleasant home, Angie. Thank you for inviting me."

"Honey, it's my pleasure," Angie said, picking up her knitting. "I want you to count this as your home whenever you're here. And I have a key for you too."

Conversation lapsed in the warmth of late evening. What the summer held, neither knew, but Diana sensed there would be a race against time. She wondered if she could do it. And would Nick be able to pull it all together?

• • •

"The end of a matter is better than its beginning and patience is better than pride," (Ecclesiastes 7:8).

four

At ten in the morning, Diana drove down Nick's gravel road and parked next to a white Jaguar convertible. The air was fresh with the smell of pines, mingled with smoke from Nick's chimney. A couple of squirrels were foraging for food. Diana pressed the bell and a minute later Nick opened the door.

"I hope I'm not too early," she said.

"Not at all." He took her jacket as she slipped it off. "Would you like a cup of coffee?"

"Yes, thank you," she said. He led her through the foyer and back to a large kitchen.

"Carol and I were just going to have a cup." He said. The redhead stood by the coffee pot. She was dressed in a jade jumpsuit, her hair coifed perfectly, her nails long and polished. _The owner of that white car._ Diana smiled as Nick made introductions and led them back to his office with the coffee tray.

"Nicky takes his black." Carol said as she took command of the tray. "How would you like yours?"

"Cream, please." Nick cleared his drawing table and spread some papers on it. Carol filled the mugs and offered Diana the cream. Taking their cups, they joined Nick.

Carol leaned close, slipped her hand through his arm, then leaned around and looked at Diana.

"I hope you don't mind my watching," she said. "I'm fascinated by what Nicky does. Just go ahead and don't pay any attention to me."

Diana resented the woman's presence. *What business is this of yours anyway?* A slow burn crept up her neck. Ignoring Carol, Nick began to describe the plans before them. Everything they discussed was there. He'd put special thought to the kitchen arrangement and provided ample room for dining. At the back of the cabin he'd made an entrance to take care of boots and coats and placed a half bath nearby in the laundry area.

"Since you've put a powder room there, would it be a big thing to add a shower and make it a full bath?"

"No, we can do that." He ignored Carol and watched Diana as he explained how that would be done. "And we'll provide for year around occupancy with heating and insulation. You could be here in winter." He looked at her for a long moment.

"I suppose that would be a good idea. There's no problem with money," she said.

"We can make it self-sufficient with an automatic

generator and propane for fuel," he said. "Sutton will watch the property."

"That's true." Carol cut in, pulling Nick around and getting into the conversation. "Sutton is like a big family. It's very reassuring," she said. Diana ignored Carol.

"When do you think we can begin?"

"This next week if the weather dries out. I'll get the excavator up there to clear it and dig the septic tank. Then I'll lay it out for the foundation. It won't happen overnight. But we'll get started." Nick began to roll up the blueprints, and Carol poured more coffee, offering Diana some. She refused. Nick joined them around the coffee tray. Carol glanced at her watch.

"Nicky, I have to run. It's after eleven, and I'm due to meet Lloyd." She looked at Diana. "It was so good meeting you. I hope we can get to know you better." She stood up. "I know where my coat is, I'll get it." She returned, and Nick helped her into it.

Diana watched as Carol faced toward Nick and kissed him. "Will I see you tonight?" she said with a little, pleading voice.

"Not tonight, Carol. I'm busy." Nick set the woman firmly away from him, both hands on her shoulders.

Visibly disappointed, Carol pouted, "All work and no play makes Nicky a dull boy." Diana watched the two as they disappeared through the hall back to the main entrance. *I'll bet they spent the night together. She sure has her claws into him...*

Nick returned smiling and Diana thought she detected a bit of relief.

"It's almost lunch. I make a mean grilled cheese. How about staying for one?" he said.

"I don't want to keep you from anything."

"You're not."

"But I heard you tell Carol that you were busy."

"I am. It's just not the kind of busy she thinks."

"Well, I'd love to since I have no plans."

He collected the coffee tray and led her back into the kitchen. It was large with lots of counter space. A dining table sat in front of a bay window, facing a grove of Aspens, with a high ridge beyond. She moved to look out on the scene, and Nick came to stand behind her. She smelled his citrus cologne and felt his breath on her hair. He did not touch her.

"It's beautiful here," she said.

"I like it. I've always lived in the mountains. I don't think I could live anywhere else."

"Have you been in this area all your life?" she said, turning to see his face.

"No, my people came from Canada, French Canadian. I was raised near the border in a lumber settlement.

"You came after I left," she said.

"Like two ships just missing each other!" He said, looking out the window, seeing and yet not seeing. It was a long moment, and he did not move. Diana had the table to her back, and she felt his closeness though they did not touch.

"Can I do something to help with lunch?" she said.

He stirred and wrinkled his nose, "Sure, are you good

at slicing cheese?" He walked over to his refrigerator and brought out everything.

As sandwiches toasted, Nick produced a bottle of chilled, white wine while Diana set the table. They sat down to hot vegetable soup, salad, and the sandwiches.

"This is lovely," Diana said. "Don't tell me you made the soup from scratch."

"No, I can't take credit for that. Mrs. Warring comes in twice a week and cleans and cooks some. But the bread is mine."

"You're kidding. You make bread?"

"See that thing over there?" He pointed to a square appliance with a glass cover. "It does it all automatically. Just put the stuff in and press a button, and four hours later you've got bread. When I was growing up, we had a cook that used to make it all the time. But the kneading wasn't for me. When this machine came out, I had to try it. I'm hooked."

"I would be too." She savored the crunchy, toasted sandwich. "You say you grew up in a lumbering settlement, with a cook? What was that like?"

"My father built a lumbering business near the Canadian border. We lived in the big house on the compound, and my mother had a cook and a housekeeper. My grandparents worried that she wouldn't survive out in that wilderness, so they supplied the servants.

"Are your parents still living?" she asked.

"Yes, they moved to Florida a few years ago. My two brothers run the company now. I'm the maverick in the group; wanted to go out on my own." Nick poured more wine and smiled. "They're great parents. When it gets too hot in the summer, they find a mountain somewhere. They usually come through here."

She watched his softened expression. There was more behind this man than she thought. Angie's account of anger and withdrawal didn't seem evident now.

"You admire your parents a lot, don't you?"

"Yes, a lot." He became silent, staring at nothing, smiling, occupied with pleasant thoughts. Then stirring from his reverie, he looked at her and said, "Now tell me about you."

Diana recounted her life in Houston, and then told him about her parents' accident. Her throat tightened as she talked about those black days. Tears welled but didn't spill, and she swallowed, not looking at Nick.

"I'm sorry, I never mean to do this when I talk about them." She smiled crookedly. "I'm in Denver now with a good firm, and I like my life. God has been very good to me."

"But how can you say God's been good when you've lost your parents? That doesn't match."

Diana breathed deeply. *In all your ways acknowledge me.*

"When I was here, I got acquainted with Mr. Sutton. We talked about spiritual things. I realized I was a sinner, and he led me to Christ. I joined the Bible study he and his wife had. I've had real peace since then." Nick stared at her.

"I'm glad for you, but that doesn't make sense to me." Sighing, she smiled at him.

"Let's do the dishes," she said.

They cleared the table and filled the dishwasher. Diana looked at her watch.

"It's getting late. I really should go." She went in search of her wrap. He joined her by the entrance.

"Have dinner with me tonight?"

"But you're busy. You told Carol—"

"I know. But have dinner with me anyway. I'll take you up to the Skyline Inn for steak. Please?" He moved closer.

"Okay." She smiled. "I can't turn down a steak dinner. I'm staying at Angie's. What time?"

"Seven?" He said, stepping closer.

"Seven." She agreed. Then he drew her to him and kissed her mouth. Catching her breath and backing away, she looked up at him, her fingers covering her mouth. "That wasn't in the contract."

"Does it have to be?" He watched her with imploring eyes.

"Hmmm... yes. I don't know you."

He released her. "I'd like to get to know you."

"But with me, kissing me is not the way. And what will Carol think?"

"Whatever she wants to think," he said, still standing close. He paused. "Did I spoil my chance for tonight? If I did, I'm sorry."

She thought a minute. "Something tells me I should accept your invitation. Tell you what, can we consider it business? I do want to get to know you better."

"If that's the only way you'll go with me, business it is."

Angie had her apron on and the vacuum cleaner was parked at her feet. Looking up from the newspaper, she said, "Hello, Honey. How'd it go? Sit down and tell me."

"Nick's plans are perfect, and he wants to get a crew up there this next week." She told Angie about adding the shower and making the cabin habitable the year round. "In fact," she added. "It's beginning to sound like a chalet."

"You've been gone almost all day."

"I know. Nick asked me to stay for lunch." Diana said.

"Really."

"Carol was there when I arrived. She left before lunch."

"Carol was there?" Angie's eyes grew wide."I thought you made the appointment with Nick. What was she doing there?"

"I don't know, unless she spent the night."

"Humph!" Angie made a face.

"She said she was fascinated by what *Nicky* did and hoped I didn't mind that she was there." Diana mimicked Carol. "I can't figure him out. She hangs on him like she owns him. He asked me out to dinner tonight, and after I accepted, he kissed me, uninvited, I might add."

"Dinner?"Angie laughed. "Carol won't like that."

"Maybe she won't find out. And anyway, it's strictly business."

"Who says?"

"I do."

"Lots of luck, sweetie. If I was twenty years younger. He obviously has come out of hibernation, so enjoy it."

"We'll see. Thanks, Angie." She picked up her purse and made her way up the stairs. She had about three hours, and she needed to unwind. Removing her suit and putting on a robe, she lay down on the bed. Nick's kiss, his arms around her, the way he looked when he asked her to have dinner, all that flooded the screen of her mind. *I must admit I'm tempted. He's smart, talented, and good-looking. But maybe I'm just another trophy. Was he testing me? Taking too much for granted? The man I want has to belong to you, Lord, and he doesn't. Help me get myself together, I don't want to go down that road without you.*

• • •

"Like a gold ring in a pig's snout is a beautiful woman who shows no discretion," (Proverbs 11:22).

ive

Nick was on time and looking good in a camel jacket and brown slacks. He was standing with his back towards her as she came down the stairs.

"Sorry I wasn't down here when you arrived," she said.

"No problem. Angie and I were talking. She just went into the kitchen… something in the oven. You look nice."

"Thanks." She smiled. "You do too."

They bid Angie goodbye and drove out of the village. Driving along, Nick seemed lost in thought. Glancing toward him, Diana was impressed by the line of his jaw and the slope of his nose. Every feature was so well balanced. *He does look very nice tonight. I wonder what he's thinking. Father God, give me the grace to be the kind of woman you want me to be tonight and for the rest of the summer too. This man is too good looking.* Nick turned and smiled.

"I hope you'll like the Inn. It's the one big attraction this area has."

"I'm sure I will. This drive is beautiful. Is it much farther?"

"Just a couple miles. When we get into the next valley, you'll see it."

The huge, old hotel was set back against the mountain and oozed the ambience of a Swiss Mountain Lodge. Stretching before it was a lush valley of grass with patches of wildflowers. They parked and Nicholas took her hand to help her up the steps to the entrance. A small, dark man in a black suit and tie came toward them.

"Ah, Nicholas, good to see you again," he said. "Jack will be sorry he missed you. He's out of town."

"This is Miss Laramore, André. We can see Jack another time. Have you got my favorite spot?" He smiled, bowed, and led them back to a secluded place.

"You must come here often," Diana remarked as they settled into a quiet booth overlooking the valley.

"I don't like to come during peak seasons, but Spring and Fall it's pretty nice. It's overrun with skiers in the winter." He grinned. "I don't ski, just cross country."

"Who's Jack?"

"Jack Danbury, the owner. I've known him for years. Whenever he's in town and I'm up here for dinner, he comes by the table. You would like him."

The waiter took their order and they settled in with easy conversation. Nick asked Diana about her work. She talked about her next project. Dinner came. *Tranche de boeuf* with red wine, spinach salad, and twice baked potatoes. It was delicious with soft music and candle glow. The evening was perfect. Nick hadn't talked much, and Diana wondered if she had been responsible for that.

When dinner was over, she said, "I'm sorry if what I said earlier today has ruined your evening. You've been so quiet."

He smiled. "Just thinking. You are really different from other women I've known."

"You mean because I didn't come on to you? I believe a relationship has to be on a friendship footing first. Kissing just gets in the way of real friendship."

"I guess I'm wondering if I've lost my touch," he said.

"Nick, this has nothing to do with you. It's me, so don't take on that kind of guilt." She bent forward, fingering her wine glass. "Your touch has nothing to do with it." The waiter came and cleared the table. Nick ordered coffee.

"Did you know W. F. well?" Diana said, as the coffee came. Nick settled back and took a deep breath.

"He was a grand, old man. I had tremendous respect for him. During the short time I knew him, we talked. He knew my father through business contacts, and sometimes I felt that he regarded me as the son he never had."

"I miss him. When I was here, I always felt he really cared for me, more than just in the work place." Diana fingered her cup and reached for the cream.

"Well, now you know he did." Nick smiled and reached across the table and patted her hand.

"And I'll do my best to fulfill his wishes." His gaze

met hers and held for a long moment. "Enough of this, would you like to dance?" he said, pulling her up.

"But..." she looked around. "Where's the dance floor?"

"Downstairs in The Cave. There's a juke box."

They passed André on the way, and Nick told him they would return, probably for some dessert. They descended wide stairs to a carpeted bar and tables with a hardwood dance area. A few people were draped around the long, curving bar, and several couples were dancing to a slow 50's melody. Nick led her to the floor. They melted together, following the rhythm, and Diana was lost in the scent of his after shave. *I must admit I like this. I like Nick too. Lord, stay close. I need You.*

It had been a long time since she'd felt this way. Or had she ever felt this way? An alarm went off in her brain, and she backed off.

"You're a good dancer," she said, smiling.

"So are you." His eyes were half closed, and he pulled her close. *Bedroom eyes...* The alarm jangled again, but Diana ignored it, enjoying the dance. Neither had noticed the petite redhead in electric blue with sparkles in her hair sitting at a far table next to a middle-aged, balding man in a gray suit. The dance ended. Nick led Diana to a table. She felt him stiffen as they noticed Carol staring at them.

"Did you finish your work, Nicky?" Carol asked, her green eyes flashing.

Ignoring Carol, he said, "Well, Lloyd, good to see you. Diana this is Lloyd Arbuckle." The balding man stood, smiled, and greeted Diana. "And of course you met Carol earlier today." Nick nodded toward Carol.

The three exchanged pleasantries while Carol silently brooded. Lloyd Arbuckle seemed gracious enough and welcomed Diana to the area, but she noticed a certain reserve about the man. Finally Carol slipped her arm through Nick's and looked up at him. "Nicky, I need to talk to you. Can we dance?"

Nick turned to Diana, "Excuse me?"

She nodded. Diana watched Nick appease Carol as he graciously led the redhead to the dance floor.

"Shall we sit?" Lloyd suggested.

"Yes, let's." Glad he didn't ask her to dance, she smiled and found a chair. Somehow she didn't trust this aloof man.

"Nick tells me you came here from New York. This must be a big change for you." She said, venturing small talk.

"Yes, it is. But I'm not here all that much. Business takes me away," he said.

"You must have a very efficient office."

"Carol is efficient, and I'm in touch every day." He smiled. "You do a lot of traveling too. Even spent time here setting up our system, I understand."

"Yes." She nodded and watched Nick and Carol. He was bent towards her listening and making a half attempt at following the rhythm. She was forceful in speaking to him, and he regarded her with condescension and for-bearance. The dance ended, and they came back to the table. Nick's jaw was rigid, and he looked stormy, but he softened when he approached Diana.

After a little more small talk with Lloyd, they said goodbye and retreated upstairs.

"Would you like some dessert?" Nick asked, taking her hand.

"No, I don't usually eat dessert." They left the Inn not saying much. He was lost in thought, and she didn't want to pry. As they headed back to St. Elmo, Diana ventured a question.

"Want to talk about it?"

"Not really. Carol can be difficult sometimes. I'm sorry you had to be a witness to that."

"Well, I want you to know I've enjoyed the evening anyway. I won't let Carol spoil a wonderful time." He reached for her hand and squeezed it.

"Thanks for that." Sighing, she hoped to elicit more from him, but they rode in silence. She wondered about the exchange on the dance floor, and she remembered the earlier incident when Carol kissed him. *She's is a beautiful woman, and what man wouldn't be interested. There must be something between them...*

They pulled into Angie's driveway, and Nick took her to the door.

"Come with me tomorrow up to the site. You don't leave for the city until later. Can I pick you up about eleven? We'll take a picnic," he said. Surprised at his insistence, she smiled.

"I'd love to, but I plan to go to church with Angie tomorrow. Maybe another time?" They walked to the door. "I meant it when I said I enjoyed the evening. Thank you for a lovely dinner," she said.

"Sure you won't change your mind about that picnic?" He bent toward her.

Diana smiled up at him. "No, but I'll take a rain check. Good night, Nick." She used her key and went inside.

At breakfast, Diana told Angie about the evening at the Inn and Carol and Lloyd being there.

"They're certainly an interesting couple. I would never put the two of them together. He's almost twice her age."

"Money! That's what makes Carol's world go round." Angie said, wrinkling her nose and sniffing the coffee in her cup. "There are some people in St. Elmo who have never gotten used to the idea that Arbuckle is CEO of Sutton. They've resented the New York class, I guess. He's definitely not one of them. It did seem strange at the time that one of the vice presidents didn't step into the position. But then, I don't know what goes on behind corporate doors." Angie rose from the table and began to clear it.

"It probably has to do with who owns what stock," Diana quipped as she carried her dishes to the sink. "Nick wanted me to go on a picnic today up at the site, but I told him I planned to go to church with you. I hope that was okay. I haven't been in church for two weeks, and I miss that." Diana said.

"I would love for you to go to church with me. I'm sure some of the people you know will be there. Do you remember John Chambers, the pastor?"

"Yes, and the Robbins. Is Ed still the police chief?"

"Ed is still the police chief, but John's wife passed away last year."

"I'm sorry to hear that. I really liked her. How has John been?"

"Okay, I think. Everyone's been very helpful to him." Angie glanced at the clock. "We should leave here about 10:30 to get there a little early."

The St. Elmo Community Church buzzed with activity, children running about after Sunday School, parishioners arriving and greeting each other. Many knew Diana and stopped to talk. It was such a friendly place. The service began with a hymn and a prayer. The choir in their robes sang, and Pastor John greeted everyone, then he called the children up for their special sermon about David and the five stones. David trusted God and only needed one stone to kill the giant, Goliath. After the last hymn, the Pastor approached the lectern, opened the Bible, and began his sermon.

"We only need one stone, the cornerstone, Jesus the Christ, who paid for our sins and is now sitting at the right hand of God. He is our high priest, speaking to the Almighty for us who believe." John Chambers, his baritone voice clear and with power, encouraged his congregation to trust their lives to Christ daily, with thanksgiving, because their sins were dealt with on the cross. "He is the perfect, sinless sacrifice that is God's means of justifying believing sinners who accept Him. Jesus Christ indwells us who believe, and together we are the building not made with hands. He is the cornerstone of our faith."

> Consequently, you are no longer foreigners and aliens, but fellow citizens with God's people and members of God's household, built on the foundation of the apostles and prophets, with Christ Jesus himself as the chief cornerstone. In him the whole building is joined together and rises to become a holy temple in the Lord. And in him you too are being built together to become a dwelling in which God lives by his Spirit.
>
> Ephesians 2:19–22

With the service over, both Diana and Angie sat quietly, thinking about those powerful words. Finally they rose and began to file out with the others. As they reached the back of the church, Nick Cureau was standing beside the last row of pews.

"Hello," he said. "After I left you last night, Diana, I thought going to church wasn't such a bad idea. So I came."

"If I'd known you were interested, I would have asked you to come along. I'm sorry."

"That's okay. I'm wondering if I can still talk you into that picnic?"

"Hmmm." She thought for a moment. "Yes, if I can change and meet you at the site."

"Sounds good." He waved at them as they passed by.

Diana was on her way from Angie's in a half hour, wearing jeans and a shirt. She draped a long-sleeved sweater around her shoulders. When she drove into the meadow, Nick was there in his truck. Getting out, he waved and walked over to her car.

"Thanks for coming, at first I didn't think you would."

"Nick, why wouldn't I? I want to get to know you, and this is a great way to do that." He went to his truck and she followed. He reached for a basket and gave her a blanket to carry.

"There's a grassy spot down by the creek, but this time of year it's still wet. So we'll pick a tree up behind that big rock. It won't be wet there." They walked up to the level area and selected a tree. From here they could see the meadow.

"This is nice. There's even a breeze." She spread the blanket, and he began to lay out sandwiches, cokes, chips, olives, and pickles, even potato salad.

"Mrs. Warring's?" Diana said, pointing to the dish. "I love potato salad."

"Yep. Help yourself," he said.

"Since we've both been in church this morning, let's have grace first."

"Sure, you say it." After thanking the Lord, they filled plates and relaxed, eating and enjoying the view.

Then Diana said, "Do you attend St. Elmo Community Church often?"

"Actually, no. I come from a Catholic background.

There's no Catholic church here, but I probably wouldn't go anyway. Just never got into the habit," he said.

"Well, I'm glad you came to SECC this morning. How did you like it?" she said.

"Chambers is a good preacher. But I didn't understand about Christ being a cornerstone. Cornerstone of what? A building? Without hands? There are lots of churches, so there are lots of cornerstones."

Please Lord, give me the right answer.

"The Bible doesn't talk about church buildings. Christ is the cornerstone of one invisible church made up of people all over the world who have accepted Him as their savior. They believe that He went to the cross and died in their place and rose again. He paid what God demands for sin, and He did it for everyone. People just have to believe they are sinners and accept what He did on faith," she said.

"Do you believe that?" he said, looking at her.

"Do you mean do I believe He did it like the Bible says, or do I believe it for myself?"

"Both."

"Yes on both questions," she said, reaching for another olive.

"What you are saying is the Bible is not a book of myths. It really happened then?" he scratched his head and swallowed a mouthful of coke.

"Yes, it really happened. Even the Old Testament. God inspired it through all the authors and preserved it to this day. The Bible is God's love letter to us." Nick was silent for a long moment.

"I'll have to think on all this. I've never heard that." They continued finishing the meal, then Nick uncovered a chocolate cake.

"Oh my goodness! My favorite. I love chocolate." Diana said. "Mrs. Warring?"

"Yep, she gets creative in my kitchen once in a while."

As Nick began to cut the cake, a shot rang out and hit the trunk of the tree they were sitting under. He dropped the knife.

"Get down flat, watch the cake, I'm going to see what that's all about."

Diana was white with fear. *Is that some kind of warning from someone who doesn't want me up here?*

Nick crawled around the tree as the sound of a vehicle roared away up on the road. Then he looked for the bullet but could not find it.

Coming back to the blanket, "I don't like this. I'll report it to Ed Robbins in the morning. It might be kids target practicing, but they should not be up here doing it. Are you all right?"

"I'm a little shaken, but I'm okay. Do you suppose someone doesn't want me up here on this land?"

"If that's true, I can't imagine who that might be. Can we finish the cake?"

Later, arriving at Angie's and packing her things, she told Angie about the gunshot.

"Probably some kids, sweetie. Try not to worry about it," Angie said. But she did worry, all the way back to Denver.

• • •

"Always be prepared to give an answer to everyone who asks you," (Peter 3:15b).

Six

Monday morning involved a staff meeting with reports on five different projects. Roger presented an overview of the work in Seattle, and it was decided that he and Diana should fly on Wednesday. This would allow time to put their plan on paper and get ready for the extended stay. Roger was exuberant. Diana dragged her feet, knowing she would have to work closely with him. She wanted to keep a professional relationship productive, but be able to declare and hold her space. Sometimes Roger smudged that boundary, and Roger probably hadn't given it a thought. He always assumed so much.

On Wednesday, the morning flight to Seattle was smooth. Roger occupied the isle seat while Diana sat by the window, both in first class. After breakfast, Roger reached over and took Diana's hand.

"I made sure our suites are next to each other. I think that will save us some working time." Diana frowned.

"Suites! Next to each other? Suites cost money, and we always have the telephone." She withdrew her hand.

"Well, the client pays for it. Why not take advantage of it?" A long, silent moment followed. "What's the matter, Diana?"

"Nothing! I just think we should really concentrate on getting the job done."

"That's why I made sure they're adjoining."

"Adjoining?" Her eyebrows shot up as she stared at him.

"Well, I'll change it if you want."

Diana became silent as the seat belt light went on, and the stewardess announced the landing approach. After the ride to Foster Development, there was a round of introductions, Roger explaining the line of command. They settled into a double work station and began to get acquainted with the company's operation.

That evening at the Seattle Sheraton, the bellhop escorted them to the third floor. Roger had requested the change from suites. However, their rooms were adjoining. *I'll have to watch that lock, or he'll be in here all the time.* Diana's face set firm lines of determination. It had been a long day, and when Roger knocked to ask if she wanted to go out for dinner, she declined in favor of room service and bed. He sounded disappointed. She ignored it... *you'll have to get used to it...*

In the morning, Diana phoned next door to see if Roger wanted to have breakfast before going to the office. He agreed and they discussed the day's work. So the tone for the time in Seattle slid into a camaraderie as the rest of that week progressed.

On Saturday, the company arranged a tour of Seattle. One of the secretaries with her husband accompanied Diana and Roger. They enjoyed the day of sightseeing, ending with dinner that evening.

Later as they entered the hotel lobby, Roger suggested a nightcap in the bar.

"I'll have a glass of wine." She said. Roger led her to a booth and went in search of the libations. Returning with her wine and his drink, he slid in beside her.

"You know, Diana, I said I wouldn't give up. We're a long way from Denver, and nobody needs to know what goes on in Seattle."

"Roger, I'm flattered by your attention, but I would know, and God would know. Doesn't that bother you? And you know what company policy is," Diana said.

"What's God got to do with it? This goes on all the time. Why not when it's what you want?" he said.

Lord, help me explain. I should get very angry, but that won't help Roger, and he needs to know. Fingering her glass of wine, Diana thought for a long minute. Roger waited for an answer to his question.

"Roger, I believe when I give part of myself away just for the pleasure of a moment, and if I do this over and over, when I come to the real relationship God has for me, there won't be much of me left." She paused and took a big breath. "You see, three years ago I met Christ. He is the Son of God, and I realized I had done that sort of thing. I am a sinner, and He saved me and made me whole again. Now I live, but He really lives in me, and I live my life to obey Him, to honor Him. That's why I can't do the things you're suggesting." Roger was silent for some time.

"I went to Sunday School when I was a kid, but I never heard that. I always thought if I didn't kill anyone or steal, or, you know, do all those Ten Commandments, I'd be okay," he said.

"And all that's commendable, Roger. But we are all born with what God calls sin, the desire to do whatever *we* want to do, and sometimes that can be doing something evil like murder or stealing. Think about your past. Hasn't there been something you've done that you're sorry about?" she said.

"Well, yes, but…" She looked up at him.

"That came from your sinful self, and you inherited that from all your forebears, just like I did from mine. It all started in the garden." She stopped and fingered her wine glass "Do you have a Gideon Bible in your room?"

"Yes."

"Read about that in Genesis 3, then read John in the New Testament. I'll pray that God will show you." She lifted her glass of wine and sipped it. There was a silence between them, and Roger didn't say more. When she finished her wine, Diana reached over and took Roger's hand.

"Thank you for the drink, and thank you for your friendship. Goodnight, Roger." She stood and left the booth, not looking behind her. *Lord, please help him to see and understand.*

In her room, she found Nick's number and dialed. She left a message on his machine with her phone number and said she would be in touch. Then she dialed Angie, who had no news about activity at the meadow.

Later, getting into bed and reaching for the lamp, the phone rang.

"Hello," she said.

"Diana, this is Nick. I hope it isn't too late. Thanks for giving me your number. I told Ed Robbins about that gun shot, and he's looking into it. I've had a crew up there digging for the water supply from the spring. The area was cleared the first of the week. The tree we ate under, that was taken down. I found the bullet and gave it to Ed," he said.

"Nick, I'm glad you've called. Thanks for the news. This week has been so busy. It sounds like you've made a good start. I could be here another two weeks, but I'll keep in touch. If you need to, leave a message and I'll return the call."

They ended their conversation, and Diana settled into bed. Her day had been a long one, and with Roger putting pressure on her for his agenda, she was stressed. *I hope what I told him is useful. Lord, help him understand.*

Sunday in downtown Seattle was a rainy day that kept Diana in the hotel. Not knowing about any church nearby, she had breakfast in the coffee shop, visited the gift shop, bought a book, and then went back to her room. She did not see Roger.

On Tuesday, Diana went to lunch with Margo, the secretary to Foster's two vice presidents. She liked Margo, and they seemed to enjoy one another's company. As they seated themselves in a nearby restaurant, Margo said, "We're going to be doing a big development in Colorado. Ever hear of St. Elmo?"

Taken by surprise, Diana said, "Yes, I have. I have friends there. What kind of development will it be?"

"As I understand, it's to be a big amusement park with a Gold Rush themed hotel and everything. Skiing in the winter and hiking, horseback riding, swimming in the summer."

"Whose land will it be on, do you know?"

"Not sure. I think it's a three way contract; a land owner, a timber company, and Foster. Quite an investment. You are lucky to live in Denver, so close."

"Well, that surely will bring jobs to the area. Sounds like a *Six Flags* idea with a Gold Rush Theme." *I wonder if that gunshot had anything to do with this? Someone not wanting me to build...*

Diana couldn't finish the day fast enough. At five-thirty she turned the key to her room. Dialing Nick's number, she waited impatiently. His deep baritone came on the line.

"Hello, Nick Cureau here."

"Nick, this is Diana. I hate to ask you, but I went to lunch with one of the secretaries today. She told me about a big development, a gold rush theme, in St. Elmo. Do you know anything about this?"

"It's not in St. Elmo. Remember the Skyline Inn? The big valley the Inn overlooks? That business venture is with Sutton and Jack Danbury, the owner of the Skyline

Inn. It's been discussed for some time. Sutton wants strict conservation agreements, and Danbury has finally come around. He's called in Foster." He paused. "Are you at Foster's in Seattle?" he asked.

"I am. I thought maybe that gunshot in the meadow might have something to do with this. You know, I keep thinking someone doesn't want me to build up there. I'm glad I was wrong, but I had to know. I hope you understand," she said.

"No new gunshots or anything else in the meadow. Trust me, I'll get your cabin built," Nick said.

"Thanks, Nick." He told her the water was piped in and that he had laid out markers for the foundation.

"Not much to see right now, but when you get back you'll see real progress." The conversation over, she prepared to go get dinner. *I still can't get that gunshot out of my mind. Nick probably thinks I'm paranoid. I guess I have to trust him.*

As Diana locked her door preparing to go for dinner, Roger came down the hall. He was smiling.

"Diana, glad I caught you. Want to go have dinner together?"

"Sure."

"I want to wash up. Can I meet you in the lobby?"

"Okay. I'll be down there."

Five minutes later he stepped off the elevator and made his way over to Diana. "Thanks for waiting." They walked to the restaurant. "I've been meaning to say I'm sorry for the way I came on to you last Saturday night. I think I understand where you're coming from." They came into the dining room and seated themselves in a booth. The waitress came and they ordered.

"So Roger," Diana said. "You understand where I'm coming from? How did that happen?"

"I took your suggestion and found that Bible. I don't entirely get it yet, but would you believe I was fascinated by Genesis. After the third chapter, I couldn't put it down. Imagine people living a thousand years. I don't know whether to believe that or not," he said. Diana unwrapped her utensils.

"I've heard some thought on that, those long-lived people were nearer to creation. Later in Genesis, God limits life to a hundred and twenty years because of the sin. And in the New Testament, it talks about the span of life as three score and ten. That's seventy years. But some have lived to be a hundred. I don't think anyone's lived beyond a hundred and twenty. You know we were created to live forever," Diana said, placing her napkin in her lap. The waitress brought their salads.

"Wow, I didn't know that. I'm hooked. I'm gonna keep reading," Roger said as he dug into his salad.

"Well, don't plan to read through the whole bible to reach the book of John. You're allowed to skip," she said. They ate in silence. Then, while they waited for the main course, they talked about the Foster work and how much longer they would be in Seattle.

"I figure my part will be finished by Friday, and I could return to Denver that evening," Roger said.

"And I probably could return a week later after doing all the finalizing and teaching. We'll know more by the time you can leave," she said, thinking about getting back to St. Elmo. *Nick said I should see some progress. I can hardly wait.*

As they finished dinner, Diana said, "Roger, I want you to know I really meant it when I thanked you for your friendship. And thank you for telling me about reading in Genesis. Do go on to John. You won't get the total picture until you do. "

Roger promised he would, and as they left the table he said, "I wonder if the gift shop has Bibles."

"No harm in asking." *Lord, keep him moving toward the flame...*

By Thursday, Roger finished his part of the Foster work, and on Friday he left Seattle. Diana, in order to finish her preparations for teaching on Monday, elected to work on Saturday. Sunday was quiet. She called Nick to check on progress. It was so good to hear his voice.

"I've laid out the markers for the foundation," he said. "I have a crew coming to dig it tomorrow. By the time you see the place, it should be ready for uprights." This pleased her.

"Have there been any more shots up there?" she said.

"No. But a distributor cap was missing from the big cat one morning when we were clearing the area. I didn't want to tell you, but since you asked, the delay was about an hour."

"Hmmm." She tried to be reasonable. "Do these things happen on a building site?"

"Yes, occasionally. We usually take it in stride. But I'll

keep Ed Robbins informed. I can't think who would not want you up here."

"Well, when I'm through here, I have some vacation time coming. I think I'll spend it in St. Elmo. Thanks, Nick. I'll see you in a week." *A distributor cap? I still think someone doesn't want me there, but Lord, I'll trust you and Nick and Ed, of course.*

Training the Foster people went well, and by Thursday, Diana felt she could leave for Denver, secure in the knowledge that the system and those who were using it worked efficiently.

Roger met her at the airport, helped with her bags, and stowed them in his car. On the way to the office, he said, "Diana, there's something I need to tell you."

"I hope they haven't got another place for me to go next week. I want to take some vacation," she said.

"No, no. This is personal. I hope you'll understand. I've been seeing Althea since I got back from Seattle. I went to church with her on Sunday, and she and I talked about Christ, about John, like you said. I accepted the Lord, Diana, and I... everything is different, changed. I have real peace about my life." She glanced at him.

"Roger, I am so happy for you. I could not be more pleased. When I accepted the Lord, someone said He would explain it to me the rest of my life. I believe that. You'll be forever understanding it," she said, a sense of joy rising inside for her friend.

"And about Althea, I asked her to marry me. I hope you don't mind." Surprised, she turned toward him as he drove.

"You hope I don't mind? I am thrilled for you both. Have you set a date?" Suddenly the thought of the apartment without Althea jogged her mind. *No Althea? Not even Osgood? New roommate? Oh, my...*

"Not yet, it kind of determines what Worthington does. I may be transferred. We're waiting to see," he said.

"Roger, I can't tell you how this pleases me. I've always known Althea admired you. Blessings on you both."

The car moved into the Worthington parking lot, and Roger transferred Diana's bags to her car while she went inside. After all the check-in business, Diana made arrangements for the vacation she planned and left for her apartment.

Althea was there, after finishing her nursing duty at three o'clock.

"I heard the great news." Diana's excitement overflowed. "I can't tell you how pleased I am for the both of you." She hugged Althea. "Do you have a ring?" Althea held out the sparkler on her left hand.

"Like it?" she said.

Diana examined the ring. "It's beautiful." *I wonder if this will ever happen to me...*

"Will you be my maid of honor?" Althea took Diana's hand.

"I would love to. Roger said you hadn't set a date."

"No, but we're pretty sure sometime this summer, depending on Worthington."

"Well, count on me."

Diana arranged with Angie to be in St. Elmo for the

evening and for the coming week of her vacation. Then she proceeded to gather her things while Osgood watched and sniffed each and everything she packed.

"Ozzy, I'm going to miss you in the days ahead," she said, scratching his neck. "Watch over your mistress while I'm gone."

• • •

"Enter through the narrow gate. For wide is the gate and broad is the road that leads to destruction, and many enter through it. But small is the gate and narrow the road that leads to life, and only a few find it," (Matthew 7:13,14).

Seven

Driving out of the city, she mused about her two best friends. She thought of Althea in a white wedding dress, and Roger nervously waiting at the altar. These two with Christ in their lives' would make a success of marriage. *If they let Jesus do the steering...*

She thought of St. Elmo and Nick, and the few times they had spent together, how he looked at her, and how he had kissed her. How that kiss had tempted her, not at the moment, but afterwards. *Lord, you've promised a way of escape. So Lord, give me that escape when I need it. And please show Nick what he needs.*

And then there was Carol. Nick just allowed her to take him over. What kind of hold did she have on him? Thinking about this and problems at the site made her head hurt. The flight in the morning, the office, then packing for the week, she was exhausted. Hearing the car, Angie came out to welcome Diana. The two women hugged and laughed, and then lugged Diana's bags into the house. Dinner was warm in the oven, the table was set, and a fire crackled in the fireplace.

"I always feel like I'm home when I'm warming myself by your fire." Diana yawned and stretched while Angie poured two glasses of wine.

"Here, sweetie," Angie said, handing her a glass. "Sit and relax a bit. We'll have dinner after while." Joining Diana on the couch, she continued, "Nick told me you found out about the big Skyline Inn development. He said he didn't know you were at Foster."

"I just never thought to tell him." Diana said, sipping her wine.

"We're all sitting on the edge of our seats wondering about it. If it goes through, it will mean more revenue for the town. But there's mixed feelings. Some think we're overrun as it is." Angie watched the fire as she fingered her glass.

"It's still pending. Things have to be worked out. Nick said Sutton wants conservation of the forest with things set in place to do that," Diana said. Both sat in silence for a long moment.

"Hungry?" Angie said, rising to go to the kitchen.

"You bet." Diana drained her glass. They ate dinner and cleared the dishes. Angie stoked the fire, and they sat until Diana could barely keep her eyes open.

It was late morning by the time she drove the gravel road to the meadow. She wanted to see for herself what had been accomplished at the site. Stopping in a neatly cleared area, she found Nick's truck alongside another older one. The white jaguar was also parked there. *Carol again. She must think it's her business.*

As she walked up the incline, Nick and a young man were examining the engine of an orange back hoe. Carol was close at hand, wearing a yellow pant suit and hovering over the two men. Carol turned.

"Diana, you'll never guess what's happened," she said, walking toward her. "Someone's removed some wiring." *Just what I need right now...*

"Hello, Carol. Do we know who did it?" *And why?*

"No," Carol said. "But these things happen all the time."

The foundation of her house was dug and set. Concrete forms still clung to entrenched cement. A load of gray building blocks had been delivered and were stacked off to the side. As she approached, the two men glanced up.

"Diana, I was wondering if you would be up here. You didn't call," Nick said.

"I've been busy. What's up with this thing?" she said, pointing.

"We're trying to find that out. It won't start. Looks like someone did it on purpose. Spark plugs are missing and some wires have been cut."

The young man raked his hand through his hair. "It was workin' last night, ma'am. I drove it off the trailer." He plopped his hat back on his head. "I'll go into town and see if I can find what we need to get her goin.' I can probably have it workin' by afternoon." Dan started off for his truck.

"Who would want to do this, Nick?" Diana said, rubbing her forehead. She felt invaded. Looking around she wondered if the perpetrator was behind some tree watching the scene.

"I don't know. It does look like someone doesn't want you to build up here. We had some trouble last week too. The big cat." Nick said.

"But these things happen all the time, Nick. You said so yourself." Carol said, adjusting dark glasses. "I'll bet there's not one building site that hasn't had something like this."

"True, but…"

Carol turned to Diana. "Now don't you worry. Everything will be okay." And turning to Nick. "I've got to get back to the office. Will I see you tonight, Nicky?"

"Probably not."

"Then maybe Sunday?" she said.

"I haven't thought that far ahead," he said, turning toward the back hoe. Carol left with what Diana thought was a huff. *She thinks she owns him, but does she?* She watched Carol get in her car and roar away, spitting up gravel.

Turning to Nick. "Do you think this is related to the gunshot?" she said.

"It might be. I'm thinking of hiring a watchman to camp up here." He backed away, wiped his hands on a rag, and turned to Diana.

She hugged herself and shivered. *Who would want to do this? What have I done? Someone must want this meadow, but for what and why?*

"Are you all right?" Nick watched her.

"I'm okay. I just wonder about everything, who, why, and that gunshot.

"Are you afraid?" he said.

"Shouldn't I be? Wouldn't you if you were me?"

"I suppose so, but that's just what they want. They'd like you to give up and leave, and I wish I knew why."

"You know, Nick, I could very well suspect you."

"Me? Why me?" Alarmed, he commanded her attention, turning her to face him. Embarrassed, Diana couldn't look at his eyes.

"Well, I understand you planned to build on this land with your fiancé. And it would be natural for you to think that I am an intruder, and that this place is sacred." Nick lifted her chin so that she looked into his face. He softened as he saw the anxiety on hers.

"I guess you need to know about Julie." He led her over to the outcrop of rock, and they sat down. "Julie was very young, too young really," he said. "She was impulsive and fun, and yes, beautiful. And I fell hard for her. She was Sutton's niece and came here from California when her mother remarried. She loved the mountains, but she also liked life in the fast lane. I was sure that I could keep her happy. I even designed a big house with what I thought would satisfy."

"The lovely painting on your wall?"

"Yes. But she couldn't stay in one place for long. I think she was always looking for something, but didn't know what it was." He grew silent staring at the ground. Diana reached for his hand.

"If it's too painful, you don't need to go on," she said.

"No. I think I should. There hasn't been anyone to talk to. W. F. knew I loved this meadow, knew that I came up here often. When we announced our engagement, he gave it to us. Julie was happy, and I designed the house, and then she got cold feet. She said she had to get away for a while. We had a fight. I didn't want her to leave, but she left anyway and went to Acapulco. The plane crashed on landing, and..." His voice cracked, and his hands closed over his face. A great well of sadness rose in Diana's chest. She remembered her relationship with Mark and how his parents killed it, she knew exactly what Nick was feeling. *This man has been through hell. No wonder he was angry.* She reached for his upper arm and gently caressed his tensed muscle.

"I'm so sorry, Nick."

"I felt guilty for a long time, like I had driven her away and caused her death. I wasn't very nice to be around, and I know W. F. was concerned. I almost became a hermit. I told W. F. that I would never build on this meadow, and since he had agreed only to signing over the land when I'd built on it, he retained the property. Then when you came along..."

"Then when I came along; I was an intrusion," Diana said.

"At first, yes. When W. F. passed away, I thought I would be somehow released from the pain and guilt of her death, but it wasn't so. Time had soothed it a bit, but I was still hurting. Then when his will included this meadow and someone named Laramore, I felt that my last shred of Julie was being taken away. I think I was even bitter about that." He stared into the distance.

"What you must have been thinking that first day when I came up here!" she said. "If looks could have killed."

"I know. I know." Nick looked at Diana and grinned. "But that's changed."

"How?"

"Well, remember that day when you came out to the house."

"Yes, Carol was there."

"After she left, you told me about your parents. I could see you were hurting, and I knew we had something in common." He reached for her hand.

She smiled. "Are you sorry you started this project, Nick? We've had some trouble."

"Sorry? No. I intend to see this thing through. I'm going to find out who's behind it. When Dan comes back I'll hire him to watch this place. I've known Dan as long as I've been here. I know his family too, and I trust him. He has his equipment up here, so I think he will have someone who can camp here too." Nick stopped and looked at her. "Now, tell me, do you still think I'm the one behind all this?" he said.

"No, of course not. I'm even ashamed that I thought it now."

"Well, don't be. It was only natural." He hopped off the rock and helped Diana down. They heard the sound of Dan's truck before it roared into view, and they walked toward it, eager to know if Dan had what he needed. The young man pulled to a stop and grinned.

"I got it all. Should work fine."

Later as they watched him work the machine, Nick turned to Diana.

"I've got some sandwiches. Are you hungry?"

"Angie pressed me with some too. I think she included a thermos." They collected their lunches and made their way over to the rock. Dan continued to work the back hoe. The hole for the septic tank grew deeper while the dirt piled higher. They ate, watching the orange machine claw the earth. Finally Dan turned it off and came to join them with his lunch.

"Should have this dug later today," he said as he opened his pail and removed a big tuna sandwich.

"Dan, do you have someone you trust to camp up here at night to guard this place so that nothing more happens? I'll hire whoever you suggest," Nick said.

"Sure. I can do it. I'll put my trailer over there," indicating a flat spot not far from the stream. "I don't want any more trouble either." He sampled his sandwich. "Okay if I bring it in tomorrow?"

Nick agreed, and he and Dan discussed the wage and how long the watch might be needed. When lunch was finished, the young man went back to his work. Diana packed up the thermos and disposed of the leftovers in a paper sack.

"I've got a crew coming on Monday to complete the foundation and pour more cement. You will begin to see progress," Nick said as he stashed the remnants of his lunch. Then he added, "Can I see you tonight?"

"I don't see why not. I'll be at Angie's. I'm sure you are welcome." Then she added, "Thanks for sharing about Julie."

"You're welcome," he said. They stood a long moment looking at each other. He was smiling slightly as he brushed a wisp of hair back of her ear. She noticed his eyes, gold flecks in brown irises. Lashes feathered his lids. She smiled at him and turned toward her car. *He is so honest, sharing about Julie. I could love this man.*

Later, while Angie and Diana were eating dinner, Diana said, "Nick asked if he could see me tonight, and I told him as far as I knew he was welcome here. I hope you don't mind."

"Goodness, no. While you were gone he was in church several times. I was never able to speak with him. Once Carol was with him." Angie reached for her water glass.

"Carol was at the site today. She assured me the cut wiring was normal," Diana said, selecting some fruit salad.

"I don't believe that," Angie buttered her role. "Three things now. Are you thinking of quitting?"

"No, I'm not ready to give up. But I do think someone is trying to get me to give up. Nick is hiring Dan to stay up there and guard the place. I thought that it might be Nick trying to get me to quit."

"Nick?"

"He told me about Julie today and the fact that he'd planned to build their home there. But that's all over. He even admitted he had become a recluse and was angry at first when he learned about W. F.'s will and me."

They finished the meal, put dishes away, and settled to watch the news. Around eight o'clock the doorbell chimed. Angie opened the door. Nick stood with two rose buds, each wrapped in lacy cellophane. "One for the hostess and one for Diana," he said, giving them to Angie.

"Come in, Nick. I'm so glad Diana invited you." She took the roses and went to find vases. Nick sat at the other end of the couch, and turning toward Diana, he angled his leg and rested it on the cushion.

"Thanks for letting me come over."

"Was there something about the building you wanted to tell me?" Angie returned with two bud vases and the roses. She placed them on either end of the mantle and turned the TV off.

"Nick, you're welcome here any time. I'm going to be in my study reading a book I've been trying to finish. I'm sure you two have things to talk over, so I'll leave you, if you'll excuse me." She whisked out of the room before either could object. Nick looked at Diana. Diana looked at Nick.

"I didn't plan this," she said.

"Neither did I. And there wasn't anything about the building that I needed to talk to you about, except to tell you not to quit," Nick said.

"Then what?"

"I don't know, except," he paused trying to find the

words, "I guess I'm curious about what makes you tick," he said.

"I'm flattered, Nick. But what makes me tick isn't really me, it's my faith in God," she said.

"How is that?" She thought for a long moment, searching for the words. And Nick waited. Finally she began, "Jesus said there are two gates, and one is very wide. The other is narrow. The wide gate is easy to go through. Lots of people go through it. But the narrow gate is where you find the Truth. He said, 'Few there be that find it.' I guess what you see is the fact that I found the narrow gate."

"How did you find it?"

Be ready always to give an answer to everyone that asks...

"I was engaged my senior year, and my fiancé broke it off at graduation. Then that summer my parents died. That put me in a real depression. I began grabbing onto anyone to replace what I lost. There were one-night stands. I tried pot. Nothing helped. Work became my salvation, but I felt so disconnected, even angry, like I had been abandoned. I had no anchor, no parents, no home, no husband. All my plans had just washed right down the drain.

"Then I was assigned to Sutton for three months. W. F. was very friendly. I think now he could see right through me. By then I knew how to put on a good front. One day he caught me when I was tired and angry. Things hadn't gone right with the system I was installing. He invited me home to dinner, and I welcomed the chance to get away from my problem. I was surprised by the peace in their home. They took my problem in stride and weren't concerned. They prayed before dinner, and it wasn't only for the food. They prayed that the problem in the system would be solved the next day. That made me blink. To me, God was something nebulous, an ancient myth out there somewhere. To think that God could solve my problem was laughable.

"When I came into work the next morning and turned on the system and brought up my troubled application, for some reason my computer stalled on one line of code. It kept coming back to it, no matter what I did. Finally I sat and studied it, and suddenly, I saw what I needed. It was like a light that went on. I fixed it and then went into W. F.'s office. It was no surprise to him, and, of course he knew God would fix it. He brought out his Bible right there in his office and showed me the promise. That where two are gathered together and ask, that it will be done. From that time I wanted to know more about this God who answers prayer. He and Annabelle invited me to their Bible Study. It was several weeks later that I became convinced that I was a sinner and needed Christ to take over my life. I've never been the same since." Nick sat for a long time.

"But that could have been just coincidence. You could have fixed it next morning anyway."

"I don't deny that, but the fact is, it did happen like that. The most dynamic part for me came along two weeks later. That one line of code just got my attention," Diana said.

"What do you mean 'dynamic part'?"

"When we studied Romans, and I saw that no one is righteous, not one, I saw myself as God saw me. I remembered the things I'd done, and I knew I was doomed. The word *propitiation,* when I finally understood it, is the sacrifice that God provided when He paid the price for my sin. All I needed to do was accept it. When I prayed the sinner's prayer, I felt the most profound peace. I can't describe it. It's never left. I was changed, and I've never looked back."

"That's pretty awesome. I've always thought of God as the creator, but He left the world to develop on its own. He's up there somewhere, just not involved," Nick said.

"I am glad you believe God created. So many people in our culture deny that."

"I've lived out in nature all my life. How one can deny a creator with all that I've seen is beyond me. Which reminds me, do you like horses?" Nick said.

"I love horses. When I was young my folks gave me riding lessons. Why?"

"I have two four-legged friends I'd like you to meet. How about riding with me tomorrow?"

"After church?"

"Yes. Meet me about two o'clock at my place. We'll ride over to the meadow along a trail. You'll really see some beautiful country."

"I'd love it."

They chatted about his horses, and where he kept them. Nick told her he planned to build a corral in the back of his home. Finally around nine thirty, Nick rose to leave.

Standing at the door, he said, "Thanks for everything. I'm interested in what you told me. I think I'll look into it. I'll probably see you at church in the morning."

"Good night, Nick." She smiled and closed the door. *My prayers go with you Nick. Lord, help him find the Truth.*

• • •

"He will teach us his ways, so that we may walk in his paths," (Isaiah 2:3).

Eight

Be still before the Lord and wait patiently
for him; do not fret when men succeed in
their ways, when they carry out their wicked
schemes. Refrain from anger and turn from
wrath; do not fret-it leads only to evil. For
evil men will be cut off, but those who hope
in the Lord will inherit the land.

Psalms 37:7–9

I'll claim that, Lord. Thank you. Diana closed her Bible,
and she padded downstairs. Angie sat at the kitchen table,
her Bible open, coffee cup in hand.

"Oh, good morning. Don't let me disturb you," Diana
said.

"No problem. I'm through with my reading and
prayers. What did Nick want last night?"

"To know why I was so different, why I didn't fall for him, I guess." Diana found a cup and poured coffee.

"What did you tell him?"

"How I found Christ," Diana said, pulling out a chair.

"Bravo, Diana. I'll put Nick on my special prayer list."

"He's invited me to go riding with him this afternoon. He has two horses he wants me to meet. Said he'd be at church today."

They had breakfast and then left for Church. Pulling into the parking lot, Diana spotted Nick's truck already there. And turning back from where they had come, she noticed Carol's white Jaguar coming up the drive.

"This should be interesting," she mumbled.

"What's interesting?" Angie said as she turned off the engine.

"Nick's truck is over there, and Carol's car is turning into the parking lot. I'm wondering what Carol will do. Today I'm just an observer." Diana smiled to herself.

They walked toward the sanctuary, meeting friends on the way. Out of the corner of her eye, Diana watched the exquisitely-dressed redhead hurry toward the entrance. People turned to look as she passed. When Angie and Diana came through the door, Carol had spotted Nick and was pushing to sit beside him. Finding seats further up front, the two women settled for the service.

Gracious God, You know I have a problem with Carol, but I do pray that the power of your Word will do a work in her life. After the hymns of worship and the children's sermon about the foolish man who built his house on the sand, Pastor John began his sermon.

"Today I want us to focus on the wise man who built his house on the rock. That rock is Christ." In deeply moving anecdotes and scriptural truth, he set out the wisdom of knowing and following Christ, finding salvation, and peace with Him.

> Therefore everyone who hears these words of mine and puts them into practice is like a wise man who built his house on the rock. The rain came down, the streams rose, and the winds blew and beat against that house; yet it did not fall, because it had its foundation on the rock.
>
> Matthew 7:24

After the benediction, they rose to go. Diana noticed Nick who was filing out. Carol was close behind. She watched Nick speak to John Chamber's at the door, and the two of them disappeared into John's study. Carol stood surprised at being left alone.

Angie and Diana moved toward Carol. "Nice to see you here today, Carol," Angie said. "Did you enjoy the sermon?"

"Yes, it was good," she said, glancing in the direction of the church study. "I wonder what Nick wanted with the pastor?"

"Answers to some questions, I suppose," Angie said.

"He may be in there a long time, Carol. We'll walk you to your car," Diana said.

Angie and Diana flanked Carol and walked with her to the parking lot, introducing her to several friends on the way, then at Carol's car, Diana said, "I'm sure Nick will call you."

"Humph. Not likely," Carol mumbled. She slammed the door and sped out, spinning her tires and spitting gravel.

"Whew. She's not a happy camper," Angie said.

"Pity the person who gets in her way," Diana said.

Around two o'clock, Diana drove into Nick's driveway. His truck was there with a horse trailer. Two saddled horses stood beside it. Nick was brushing them and feeding them carrots from a nearby bag. She parked by the trailer and got out of her car.

"Hello," he said. "Come meet my friends."

"Nick, they're beautiful." Walking easily, she said, "Tell me about them."

"This is Champ," he said, offering a carrot. "I've had him for two years." Nick stepped closer and patted the big animal. He was a handsome bay, and Diana stroked his neck. "Champ, this is Diana. See, she likes you already." The horse nodded and whinnied, pawing the ground.

"He knows," said Diana, moving closer to Champ. The animal nuzzled Diana's hand.

"And this is Belle, Champ's stable mate. I've had her since last fall." Nick moved to give her a carrot. "Belle, meet Diana. She likes you too." The brown filly with a beautiful, black mane accepted Nick's carrot and eyed Diana.

Nick rubbed her neck and Diana said, "Hello, Belle. Can I rub your neck too? Nick, they are beautiful. Tell me a little bit about them."

They stood rubbing and feeding the animals, while Nick gave a brief history of each. Then he said to the horses, "You guys want to go?" They both whinnied in unison. Nick helped Diana into Belle's saddle, then mounted Champ. "We'll ride around back. The trail starts there, so follow me." She watched him sit easily on the horse, becoming one with the animal.

They rode through a cleared area in back of Nick's home to the beginning of a trail that wound through forest and boulders. Wild flowers grew in isolated spots. The trail sloped upward, winding eventually in a switch back pattern. At the top of the ridge, Nick reigned Champ, and Diana stopped beside him.

"It's beautiful up here," she said.

"I wanted you to see the view," he said, pointing. "There's Sutton over there, and to the right you can see St. Elmo. I love to ride up here and get my head straight."

"I can see this is perfect for that."

They sat in their saddles and gazed at the vista. Nick pointed to the peaks and named them, indicated the direction of the Skyline Inn, and then pointed down the other side of the ridge.

"Your meadow is down there, and I thought we could ride down and see if Dan has moved in. That is if you are good for the ride."

"I'm good. I may have to use liniment tonight, but let's go."

They rode single file over the ridge and winding down through boulders, aspens and pines eventually coming on the site from behind. Nick showed Diana the spring where water was piped down to her building. Dan had pulled his trailer into a cleared space and had hooked up his water line to the outlet. As they rode towards the camp, Dan came out and hailed them.

"Hello. Tie up and sit a spell," he said, setting up some lawn chairs.

"We'll do that," Nick said, dismounting. "Everything okay here? Do you have everything you need?"

"I'm goin' in town later to get Duke, my German Shepherd. Best watch dog I've ever had. He'll be good company too. Can I get y'all a coke? I've got some in my cooler." Both nodded and Dan went to his cooler. Diana noticed Dan's shotgun leaning against the trailer beside his cooler. *I hope he won't have to use that...*

"As soon as we get electricity in here from the main road, we'll hook you up. Should be a couple of days." Nick said.

"Dan, I really appreciate that you are going to be here," Diana said, popping her coke can.

"Aw, that's okay ma'am. I can fish all I want while I'm here. It's like vacation."

As they sat, Nick explained his schedule. Logs would be delivered from the sawmill by the end of the week, and in the meantime, the foundation would be finished and cement would be poured.

"And I'll be around here every day to see about things," he said.

Finally they mounted the horses, said goodbye to Dan, and started back the way they came. When they arrived back at the truck and trailer in Nick's driveway, Diana dismounted.

"Nick, can I help you put them in their stable?"

"You really want to?" He turned, surprised, and looked at her.

"Yes. I always used to do that after a ride." Nick led each horse up into the trailer, secured the door, and directed Diana to the passenger seat in his truck. As they moved up the driveway, he said, "Julie was never interested in my horses. I could never figure out why."

"I'm sorry, Nick." She watched him noticing his set jaw. They turned onto the road and Nick described the corral and barn he planned to build.

"Want to get it done before summer is over. That way I can keep an eye on them and ride more often."

Soon they pulled up to Shady Stables. Nick and Diana led the horses to water and then into the barn. Nick removed the saddles and bridles while Diana found a brush. She began to work over Belle. Nick put fresh hay out for both and commenced to rub Champ with an old towel. In about twenty minutes the job was done. After the trailer was parked and unhitched, they started back to Nick's place.

"You really knew what you were doing in there," Nick said.

"Putting your horse away properly was required as

part of the riding lessons. I really enjoyed it, and I often earned extra money helping to clean out the stables," she said.

Nick smiled and shook his head, "I'm impressed."

Turning off the highway onto Nick's drive, they spotted a white jaguar parked beside Diana's car.

"Well, guess who," Nick mumbled. He took a big breath and let it out slowly. As they parked his truck, Carol hurried from the house.

Perfectly dressed and coifed, she said, "Nicky, did you forget you're supposed to take me to dinner?" Then spying Diana, "Oh, hello Diana," a frown crossing her face. As Nick got out, Carol wrapped her arms around him to kiss him. "Whew, you smell like a stable. Those awful horses." And she backed away.

"Carol, I had no plans to take you to dinner. You must have gotten mixed up somehow," Nick said.

"I thought we could talk about what you and John Chambers talked about at church today," Carol said in a whiny voice. "After all, you work for Sutton, and Lloyd needs to know." Nick faced the redhead.

"I am employed at Sutton, but I don't remember anything in my contract that says my off hours belong to Sutton," he stated, visibly annoyed. "Has Lloyd sent you to spy on me?" Diana was speechless, watching this exchange.

"Oh no, Nick." Carol moved toward Nick and visibly softened. "Of course not. I just thought... Nicky, you know, I really care about you and—"

"Thanks, but no thanks." Nick turned and came around his truck to help Diana down.

"I'm sorry, Nick," Diana said quietly, not intending that Carol should hear. "I hope this won't jeopardize you and Sutton."

"Carol's overstepped. It's been coming on for some time." Ignoring Carol, Nick led Diana over to her car.

"Thanks for riding with me and putting Champ and Belle away," Nick said.

"Nick, I loved it. Thanks for inviting me."

Nick leaned closer. "I would like to kiss you—"

"Please don't. I don't want to get involved with—," she nodded toward Carol.

"I understand. Thanks. See you tomorrow at the site?"

"Yes, probably." Diana drove off, peering in her rear-view mirror. Body language of both Carol and Nick looked like an argument. *Hmmm. Hold the line, Nick. I also wonder what you and John talked about. Lord, I pray Nick finds You. Work in his heart and draw him to Yourself...*

• • •

"Everyone who does evil hates the light, and will not come into the light for fear that his deeds will be exposed," (John 3:20).

*N*ine

Monday, mid-morning, Diana packed a lunch and took it out to the meadow. As she drove into the area, men were working around the foundation, others were laying pipe. Dan and his dog, Duke, were on hand, and Dan invited Diana to sit under his awning.

"So, this is Duke." Diana reached over to pat the big Shepherd. "He's a beautiful dog, Dan." The animal waged his tail and licked Diana's hand. "He likes me," she said.

"Duke's a good boy. We had no trouble last night, Miss Diana."

"I'm glad to hear that. Has Nick been here?"

"He was this morning early. Said he'd be back before lunch."

"You know, Dan, I think I'll walk around the meadow. I need the exercise, and when I get back, Nick will probably be here. Tell him I brought my lunch," Diana said.

"Want to take Duke with you?"

"Will he go with me?"

"He will on his leash."

Diana squatted down on Duke's level. "Duke, will you go walk with me?" The dog began to bark and prance around while Dan put the leash on his collar.

"There he is, Miss Diana. Duke, you take care of her."

The two started out, Duke walking beside Diana.

"Duke, you have been to obedience school, I can tell. What a good boy." The dog looked up and wagged his tail.

They walked at an easy pace. The road curved close to the meadow, then circled around, and through the forest at its edge. Tall pines towered over patches of mountain laurel with wild flowers tucked in the bright spots. Diana luxuriated. *Lord, this is Your place, Your country. Help the building, show me what You want here.*

About a mile where the meadow narrowed and the road began to turn, Duke suddenly stopped. He growled quietly looking up into the forest. Diana turned to see why he was growling. High up, she saw a man standing, watching looking through binoculars. When he realized she saw him, he turned and hurried on out of sight.

"Well, Duke, I wonder what he was doing around here. Maybe Sutton? We'll ask Nick when we get back." They walked on, faster now with the intruder in mind.

As they reached the clearing, Nick was there, his truck parked next to Diana's car. He hailed them.

"Hello, Dan said you went walking."

"Nick, do you know if Sutton has someone doing anything in the area, the forest at the end of the meadow?" Diana said.

"No, not that I know of. Why, did you see someone?"

"Yes, Duke growled, and I saw a man up in the pines at the end of the meadow. He was wearing fatigues and looking through binoculars. When he realized I saw him, he disappeared."

"I'll look into that at the office. It's possible Lloyd had someone surveying in the area." Nick looked around then glanced at his watch. "It's time for lunch. Dan said you had yours."

"Let me take Duke back to Dan, then I'll join you," Diana said as she moved toward the trailer with the dog.

Later, on the outcrop of rock, they spread their lunches.

"Nick, that man still bothers me. Do you know what's off in that direction?"

"No, I don't. We'll have to wait and see what Lloyd says."

"Was Carol okay after I left yesterday?" Diana said.

"It took a while, but she left, and I did not take her to dinner. By the way, I apologize for wanting to kiss you in front of her. I wanted to make a statement. That was selfish of me."

"Carol's not someone I would care to cross," Diana said.

"Well, I crossed her yesterday. And I think I can handle her. By the way, John gave me C. S. Lewis' book, *Mere Christianity.* Have you read it?" Nick said.

"Uh huh. A couple of years ago." Diana bit into a pickle.

"I settled down with it last night," Nick said. "He sure explains how people are. Even if we have good intentions, we can't carry them out."

"Have you come to the *Hound of Heaven* yet?" Diana asked.

"No. John loaned me a Bible. I've got to get up to the bookstore and buy my own."

"You're in for a great adventure." *Lord, show him.*

They continued eating in silence. As they finished, a cement truck bumped into view, and they watched as the men prepared to pour the floor.

"We'll be able to put logs in place soon." Nick said, "Then you'll see real progress."

Tuesday and Wednesday progressed much as had Monday, with Diana and Nick eating their lunches and watching the workmen. Nick had asked Lloyd about the man Diana had seen. Lloyd had ordered no surveying.

"It might have been someone from the National Forest," Nick said, as they finished lunch." He could have been unaware of the boundary, and when he saw you, figured he'd come too far."

Wednesday evening, Angie and Diana were watching the TV when the announcer broke in with a live news flash. The Pine Mountain Sawmill was on fire. Equipment from three districts had been called. Two were on hand. The television crew could not get near the flames, but were interviewing a firemen who had information.

"I can't say how much was lost at the mill. We're try-ing to contain it from getting away into the forest."

"I'll bet that's where your logs come from." Angie said as the two watched with wide eyes.

"Do you think so?

"Pine Mountain is an hour from here, and I know they supply most of the builders around these parts," Angie said.

"I wonder if Nick is watching this," Diana said. They continued to watch the report. When the news switched to other things, the telephone rang. It was Nick.

"I suppose you know about the fire?" he said. "I wish I'd had your logs delivered today. I'll get out there in the morning with Sheriff Robins. Then on Friday, do you want to go out there with me?"

"Yes." *More trouble,* she thought, pressing her temple and closing her eyes.

"Good, I'll pick you up at eight. See you on Friday."

The sun glinted through thick pines as they drove along the mountain road. The snow was gone now, and the aspens had greened out. Spring was becoming sum-mer, and time was passing swiftly.

"Nick, do you suppose this fire has anything to do with my cabin? We both agreed it looked like someone didn't want me there," Diana said.

"It looks like it. Yesterday Ed was certain about arson. He's going to be out here today too."

I wonder if I should give up. This isn't worth getting the forest burned and a business destroyed.

They rode on in silence, then Diana asked, "Nick, what's it like on these roads in the winter?"

"This one isn't used much, closes down when the big snows hit, but the main highways are kept open. You'll be able to get to the cabin okay. Plows keep that road open. You'll want to lay in a good supply of food and wood though. It could take the plows as much as twenty-four hours to get though. You've got to remember my place is off the same road. I have the same problem. That's why I have a ham radio set up. We'll have to get you fixed with something besides a phone. The lines can go down. You might want a four-wheel drive vehicle too."

"You mean like a Jeep?" she said, wide eyed. Diana hadn't thought about this.

"Don't worry about the expense," Nick countered. "W. F. probably thought about that. He thought about everything." He settled back and glanced at her. "I'm beginning to think he put us together on purpose." He laughed. "He was a pretty good judge of character, and I'll bet it pleased the old man to try to get us together. He's probably up there smiling right now."

"But that doesn't make sense, Nick. Julia was his own flesh and blood, and he must have really wanted you together. Don't you think you just got this duty because you're part of Sutton?"

"Maybe so, maybe so." And they rode along until Nick turned into the yard of the sawmill.

Already, workmen were rebuilding the burned part of the business. The blackened and charred logs in the yard were a sorry sight. She noticed the fire had spread to the rise behind the buildings. The ghosts of tall trees stretched naked toward the blue sky.

"How sad," she said.

"See that charred stack of logs over there? The blackest ones and the most destroyed?"

"Yes?"

"Those were yours. You can figure that someone got up there on top and poured gasoline all over them, then got down and doused around the logs, and set it afire. It looks like they were picked out of all the rest. You can see where the fire jumped to the building and then beyond."

"Someone doesn't want me in that meadow," Diana mumbled, dread overtaking her.

"We'll talk to Ed."

Five minutes passed while they watched the activity. Robbins arrived and parked his car beside Nick's truck. As they walked toward the yard, Ed pointed here and there, explaining what happened when he first arrived on the scene. He had a good idea when the fire had been set. Then he launched into the findings of the investigation so far.

"We're talking to all the employees here. There's one we haven't been able to contact. Seems he's out of town, but we're trying to locate him for questioning."

"What's his name?" Nick asked.

"Name's Matt Bonar. He's only been around about four months and just started to work here this season. We're running a background check on him. It will take some time to get that back. When that comes in, we may know something. Meantime, hang in there, Miss

Laramore." The affable middle aged man smiled encouragement. "And let us know if anything more happens," He added. They stood watching the workers. Nick and Ed continued to talk.

Diana wandered over where her blackened logs were. The sight made tears come to her eyes. *Why would someone want to do this?* She stared for some time and then returned to the men. Nothing more could be done, so the three walked back to the vehicles.

As Nick started the engine and moved out of the yard up to the road, both were silent. A cold chill crept over Diana. She remembered the gunshot, the distributor cap, a filter, the spark plugs, the strange man, and now this. *My logs were specially targeted! Who would want to keep me out of the meadow, and want it so badly that they would deliberately start a fire?*

"Nick, I'm frightened," she finally said. He glanced at her as they moved along the bumpy road.

"Can't say I blame you. Someone wants something awfully bad, bad enough to do what we just saw. It's time for lunch. Are you interested?" Diana sighed.

"I suppose I could convince myself to eat something."

"We just have to give Ed time for his investigation. So let's put all that on the back burner. There's nothing we can do about it now, and everything is under control. Besides, I'm hungry, and we're not far from the Inn. Remember Jack Danbury? He just might be there this time."

When they arrived, Nick led her through the entrance. They were greeted by a tall, distinguished man. Traces of gray etched his dark brown hair. Jack Danbury laughed aloud when Nick introduced him as St. Elmo's next mayor.

"Don't know about that," he replied. "I haven't decided to run yet. We're looking for a decision on that development project, and if that goes through, I expect to be very busy."

"Any idea when that might be?" Nick asked.

"Seattle's ready to go with it, but there's a bit of a snag with Sutton. Details of the contract, I think. That should be refined next week."

"Sutton won't do anything unless conservation measures are spelled out and an inspection schedule set in place. That's what's holding it up," Nick said.

"Well, you two would like some lunch I'll bet." Jack smiled, and led the way to Nick's favorite table. The rest of the dining room was busy with every place occupied. "We saved it for you," he said as he seated them. "Enjoy your lunch." Smiling, he departed, and a waitress brought menus.

"I like him," Diana said, opening the menu.

"Jack's a good friend. He works hard and always has everyone's best at heart."

They ordered lunch, and when the waitress left, Nick said, "When Jack's development goes through; he's going to need someone to set up a computer network. I think you're just the person for the job." Diana smiled.

"Working with Jack is a tempting thought, but right now I'm not sure I should try to finish in the meadow."

Nick gasped, "Of course we'll finish. Don't tell me

you're thinking of quitting? We'll get to the bottom of this." He unrolled his utensils. "I intend to call my brother in Canada and order more logs. That will delay us a couple of weeks. We should have plenty of time before snow falls." The waitress returned with lunch.

"Well, I will pray about it." Diana said, forking her food. "I have to be sure God wants me to go ahead on the cabin first." They ate in silence. *Lord, Nick seems so sure about all this. Help me to know what you want me to do.*

Finally, her lunch almost gone, Diana said, "You know, Nick, I can't help thinking that there is so much good that can come out of finishing my cabin. And I guess I shouldn't let this trouble stop me, because I'm coming to see this opposition as evil. Does that make sense?"

"I know," he said. "I've been thinking that too. I might do some investigating on my own. I've got a few angles I might look into."

"Like what?"

"Right now I'd rather not say in case I might not find anything. But you can bet I'll tell you if I do." They finished lunch and said goodbye to Jack. Driving back to town, they talked about the fire and wondered about the person who set it.

Arriving at Angie's, Diana curled up on the couch. Her mind wandered to W. F. *I wonder if he thought Nick and I would be good together. He was wise, and God was with him. He knew what I needed. Lord, your Spirit was working in him, and now in me. O Father, do a work in Nick too. Show us what's happening. Give us wisdom. I love you, Lord.*

Diana had dosed off when Angie came through the door. The clattering in the kitchen woke her. She stretched and went to see Angie.

"Dear me, girl," Angie said. "I didn't even notice you there. The lights weren't on. I just thought you hadn't come in yet."

"Nick took me out to the sawmill. It's a sad sight, Angie. You know it really scares me. You could see that my logs were the ones targeted. They were completely demolished. Someone got up on top and poured gasoline all over them." Angie stood still and listened, frowning as Diana talked.

"Did Ed have any clues as to who might have done it?"

"No. Except he did say they had not been able to question one of the sawmill employees. He's out of town or something. Said his name is Matt Bonar. That's all I know."

"Well, honey, try not to worry. Ed will keep on 'til he gets all the answers." Angie laid out dishes and silver and removed the lid to her crock-pot. The aroma was tantalizing. She placed a salad along side the stew and completed the meal with crusty, garlic bread and sweet tea. Diana watched. *Angie is so dear to do all this.*

"Angie, this looks wonderful." Diana hadn't realized how hungry she was. The two filled their plates and gathered around the coffee table to watch the news on TV. After the world report, the announcer talked about the craft fair, officially called Elmo Days, scheduled to open tomorrow. Then he gave an updated report on the fire and an interview with Ed Robins. Matt Bonar was wanted for questioning and anybody having any information about his whereabouts was asked to call the Sheriff. As his picture flashed on the screen, Angie gasped.

"I've seen that man. He was in the library a while back. He got a card and asked to see some books on local history. He seemed kind of angry that he couldn't check them out. We don't let volumes from our research shelves leave the library. I didn't pay much attention to his name."

"Well, that's interesting," Diana said. "I think Ed would like to know that. And for that matter, I'll bet Nick would too." Diana called Nick and told him what Angie had said.

"Put her on the line," he said.

After Angie hung up, she said, "Nick wants to know if I can find the books Bonar wanted to check out. He'll meet us at the library tomorrow morning around nine. Maybe there's something in those books, if I can remember which ones." Both women looked at each other, awed by the mystery. Later it was hard for Diana to end her evening when the time came. Before retiring, she picked up her Bible. Turning to the second chapter of Peter, she read this:

> For if God did not spare angels when they sinned, if He did not spare the ancient world when He brought the flood, if He condemned the cities of Sodom and Gomorrah, and if He rescued Lot, if this is so, then the

Lord knows how to rescue godly men from trials and to hold the unrighteous for the day of judgment, while continuing their punishment.

2 Peter 2:4–9

• • •

"In all your ways acknowledge him, and he will make your paths straight," Proverbs 3:6.

Ten

Angie and Diana arrived at the library to find Nick waiting on the steps. He greeted them and then eagerly asked, "Can you remember what it was he wanted?"

"I think it had something to do with old mines," she said as she unlocked the door. "You know the area is dotted with them. They're mostly all played out. But once in a while someone gets the idea that it's not really so, and they come in here and pour over these books." She led them to a shelf in the research section.

"Thanks, Angie. Any of these look familiar? I know that was a while ago." Nick began browsing the shelf. Angie pulled down several volumes, one that she remembered, and then pointed to another.

"That one is a good possibility too." Nick took the volumes.

"Look," he said. "Weren't you two planning to go over to the fair for a while? Since the library is closed today, and I'll need some time to look, why don't you ladies run along. When I'm through, I'll come over and find you."

They agreed, and Angie locked Nick inside with instructions to secure the door when he finished. The two women crossed over and moved toward the craft booths on Main Street. Activity was beginning with people gathering, greeting each other, and looking at the various handmade items. Diana recognized a few people. Mrs. Robins, Ed's wife, was there, and she and Angie stopped to chat.

"My dear," she turned to Diana. "I'm so sorry about the fire. Ed told me. I hope they find who did it soon." Diana thanked her. They walked on slowly, examining the pretty things in each booth. One lady displayed lovely, braided rugs. Diana especially liked one with shades of blue and green, and she asked her if she could make a large one to fit a specific room size.

"Oh yes," she said, smiling. "It takes a while for a big one, so you need to give me an order. Here's my card. Just let me know the size you want and the colors."

They walked on and came to a stall with handmade rocking chairs.

"Oh, Angie. Imagine one of these by my fireplace. I'd put a colorful, gingham pillow seat on it and maybe a matching one at the back." Diana traced the fine finish on the rocker.

"Sometimes," Angie said. "We see something, and we can't have it because the circumstances aren't there. Why not take this man's card? I'm sure he's got one." So Diana collected another card. She was equally impressed with the quilts and the afghans. There were handmade dolls of all descriptions, both rag and porcelain, various stitched items, wood-painted things with a country theme, silver, Indian jewelry with inlays of onyx and turquoise, leather belts, and silver buckles, a booth with jams and jellies, and on, and on, and on.

It was close to noon when Diana felt a hand on her elbow as she leaned over to examine the details on a large piece of antique lace. She turned to find Nick grinning down at her.

"Hi. Find something you like?" His eyes had a curious light in them, and his smile told her he liked what he saw.

"Nick," she breathed, watching him. "This is over a hundred years old. It's beautiful. It's handmade. I've never seen anything like it." She touched the delicate piece. "I guess I'm just old-fashioned. I love to look at things like this. I don't think these old things will be around much longer. Everything's done by machine and computers now." She sighed. Nick leaned down and kissed her cheek very lightly. "Why did you do that?" she said quietly.

"Because you see beauty and you want to preserve it, and I like that about you."

"Oh," she smiled up at him.

"Now," said Nick. "We are going to find Angie and give her a library report. We have some things to do and places to go." Diana looked around.

"There she is, over by the antiques." They approached Angie, who was examining a crystal, butter dish.

"Look what I found," she said. "Oh, hello Nick." She replaced the dish. "Did you find anything helpful?"

"Possibly," Nick said. "We'll have to check it out. I'm commandeering Diana. I hope you don't mind. I'll bring her back to your house later." They said goodbye.

"Where are we going?" Diana asked, falling into step as they walked.

"We're going to see Jake McKibbon."

"Why Jake McKibbon?"

"There's an old, abandoned gold mine on what I think is your property. The account calls it the Old McKibbon Mine. I want to know if Jake is connected in some way."

"Wouldn't W. F. have known about it?"

"Not necessarily. It was worked in the late 1870s and was abandoned by 1890. According to the record, it never brought in much. W.F. was into wood products and forest management. Old mines were regarded as worthless, and most of them still are. Jake might tell us something about its history. Mind walking the three blocks over to the Carter Hotel?"

"No."

They hurried past the fair crowd, taking a side street toward the hotel. They walked through the ornate, etched, glass doors. Jake looked up from his station with a twinkle in his eyes, brows arched as he peered over his glasses.

"Well, I see you two have met." He grinned as they approached his desk.

"Jake can we talk to you for a bit?" Nick leaned on the counter.

"Sure can. Come on around to the back room here. I can hear anyone who rings my bell." The wizened, old gentleman led them into a small sitting room with tall, narrow windows. A large desk and books lined one wall. He offered them the Victorian divan, and he took the chair at his desk. "I hide out in here when things are slow. Now, what can I do for you two?"

"We need to know about the Old McKibbon Mine."

"Now that's very interesting," Jake said. "Nobody's asked me about that place in years. And three weeks ago someone was in here wanting to know all about it."

"Know who he was?"

"Nope, can't say as I've ever seen him before. He was a tall fellow, black hair, had a different way of talking." Jake leaned back in his chair, putting his hands back of his head. "You know, Will Sutton and I grew up together. We became friends when his dad bought that old mine from my dad. By that time, the place was abandoned. My grandpa worked it, didn't get much gold out of it, and passed it on to Pa. Pa needed the money and was glad to sell it. But Sutton wasn't interested in minerals, just trees and lumber products, so it's not been worked all these years."

"What did this guy want to know?"

"How to get to it. Said he was a rock hound, amateur collector on vacation."

Nick told Jake about Diana's inheritance, the stipulations involved, and that he was fairly certain the mine was on the property that would be hers. He didn't mention the trouble they'd had at the site. Jake was pleased that Diana would be spending more time in St. Elmo. He offered any help he could and said he'd let Nick know if the 'rock hound' showed up again. They left the old man and walked to Nick's truck.

"Are you getting hungry?" Nick asked.

"Hmmm. Yes. I could eat something."

"How about a Big Mac? I'll do the drive-though, and we'll take them with us." After they picked up lunch, they took the road to Nick's place and passed the turn off to her meadow.

"Ever been this far along here?" Nick glanced at Diana.

"No. What's up here?"

"You'll see in a few minutes." Soon the road began to diminish to thin gravel and further to scrubby, rough terrain. Nick drove through as much as he dared and then pulled to a stop. "We'd better eat lunch now before we go hiking around that ridge." They rolled down windows and spread out the cheeseburgers and cokes. "If you look closely, you can see a semblance of a path through that ravine. It goes up onto that ridge. I've never followed it, but I assume the old mine is at the end of it." They both ate lunch and gathered their wrappers.

"Nick, my shoes aren't fit for hiking. I need something a little more sturdy than these things." She looked at her patent-leather flats.

"We'll go as far as we can. We might be able to sight something before we need to turn back." He gathered his camera and binoculars. "If we meet someone that wonders who we are, we'll just be tourists," he said, handing Diana the camera to carry.

They followed a path through the trees. The air was fresh with pine. The sun was directly overhead and a pleasant breeze fluttered the aspens. A bee buzzed around them and darted off toward some mountain roses. After about ten minutes of steady hiking, they heard the rush of descending water, cascading over boulders in a stream. They followed the winding path, and it finally ascended up onto a ledge above the trees. Here it became danger-ous, for parts had disintegrated with winter snows and the passing of time.

"This is about as far as I think we'd better go," Nick said. He removed his binoculars, adjusted, and peered through them at the area they wanted to see. Diana watched him as he searched the side of the mountain along the rim.

"There. I think I see something," he said. "It looks like a rugged hole in the cliff, like a cave maybe." He handed Diana the binoculars. "If you follow the path carefully and get to that darker patch of mountain just above those trees." He pointed in the direction for her to see. She did as he suggested and found the cave.

"I see it! How do we know that's the mine?" She began adjusting the fine sight. Then she saw something, or she thought she did. "Nick, there's someone there. Here, look." By the time he adjusted it to his eyes and found the cave again, it was gone.

"Are you sure you saw someone, Diana?"

"Well, where the cave was black, there was suddenly

the form of a man standing there. I couldn't make out anything more. I wonder if he saw us. Is there a way into that mine from the other direction?" she said.

"Yes, it's a two hour ride around the mountain, and you have to come in from Leadville. I'll try to get over there this next week." They returned to the truck, each of them thinking about where they'd been and what Diana thought she'd seen. By now it was late afternoon.

"Promise me something." He said, turning toward her and placing his hands on her shoulders so that she leaned against the truck. He looked full in her face.

"What?"

"That you won't worry about this mine or think about what you saw?" he said.

"That's easy for you to say. It's you I'll worry about when you make that trip to check it out. Personally, I hope I was mistaken." He raked his hand through his hair.

"I don't know what's so dangerous about checking out that mine. If I find someone, I'll just tell them I'm from Sutton, checking out the land." He helped Diana into his truck.

"Well," she said. "I will pray that you will be safe. If someone is up to no good, they could be carrying guns."

Coming around to the driver's side, he said, "What makes you think prayer would protect me from guns?" He climbed in and faced her.

"Well, I have faith in the Lord. He will see to it that you won't face a gun. Which reminds me, have you got your own Bible yet?" Diana said.

"Haven't had a chance." Nick started the engine and backed around to get to the road. "Want to go to the bookstore with me? I think we'll have time before it closes."

"Sure." They drove back to town and parked on the street in front of the bookstore. Entering, the clerk greeted them and Nick said, "I'd like to see some Bibles."

"Do you have a particular translation you'd like?"

"The one I'm using is the King James Version." The clerk brought out several leather-bound Bibles, explaining about each one.

"You might find this New King James a good choice." He said. Nick picked it up and opened it, studying the print and the notes, the helps and the concordance. Then he looked at Diana.

"What do you think?"

"That is a very good translation. It's very close to the one you have been reading. Just removes the old English and makes it more understandable for today," she said. "And look, it's been tabbed so you can find the books."

"I'll take it," Nick said. The clerk rang it up. As they left, Nick said, "I'll return John's Bible tomorrow. Glad you asked me about this."

"Do you remember where you've been reading?" she asked.

"Actually, no. I've been in *Mere Christianity*. Do you have a suggestion?"

"Yes. The book of John."

As they drove into Angie's driveway, she came out to the truck.

"Well, I'm dying to know what you found in those books," she said.

Getting out of the truck, Nick said, "We talked to Jake McKibbon about his dad's old mine. Seems the same fellow that was in the library went to ask him how to get there. We went as far as we could on the old trail and looked through binoculars. Diana thought she saw a man in the opening of the mine."

"I could have been mistaken, but he was so clear," Diana said.

"Oh, my goodness." Angie put her hand over her mouth.

"Now ladies, I don't want you to worry. I intend to check it out as soon as I can. I've got to replace the logs we lost in the fire. First chance I get, I'll drive around there and check it out." Nick made them both promise not to worry. He got back into his truck, waved, and drove off.

"We just came from the bookstore where Nick bought a gorgeous, leather-bound Bible." Diana said as they walked toward the house. "I hope he's going home to read it."

"We'll just pray that he will."

• • •

"All over the world this gospel is bearing fruit and growing" (Colossians 1:6).

Eleven

The trip to Denver was uneventful. Diana left St. Elmo, wishing she could stay the rest of her life. She arrived at the apartment late Sunday afternoon. It was empty except for Osgood. His tail held high, he greeted Diana with purrs of love and a rub on her leg as she set her bags on the bed.

"Hello, Ozzie, where's your mistress?" Diana scooped him up and gave him a chin rub. "Doesn't look like she left me a message." She released him and turned to unpack her bags. The cat watched everything, and at one point, climbed into the empty case. *You are such a nice kitty, Osgood. I'll need one just like you after you move.* Later as she lay on the couch watching the news, Nick called.

"Just wanted to know if you got back okay," he said.

"I did. Althea isn't here, just Osgood. He purred and greeted me with a rub. I think I'm going to have to have a kitty. Did I tell you about Althea and Roger?"

"No, I don't recall."

"Well, they're engaged, and the wedding might be soon. She wants me to be a maid of honor. I may not get back there soon, Nick."

"Everything's under control here, but I'll miss you. I kind of like having you here." She laughed.

"I like being there too. But I'll know more when I see them." They talked about the weekend, and the old mine. He expected the shipment of logs would be delivered in two weeks. In the meantime, Dan would stand by. Ed Robins would be completing his investigation. She urged Nick to be careful when he went to investigate the place.

"You know, sweet lady, I like it that you are concerned for me."

"Why shouldn't I be concerned for you?"

"Well, it just tells me I've become important to you, and I like that." She knew he smiled into the phone. "By the way, I still think you need to send your resume to Jack. He's going to need someone like you," Nick said, changing the subject.

Saying goodbye, she hung up the phone, turned off the TV, and gave Osgood a rub.

"And I've got to go to bed, Ozzie. We're not sitting up to wait for your mistress. C'mon." The cat followed her into the bedroom and stretched himself at the foot of her bed. Diana flipped off the light. *Hmmm, he likes it that he's important to me. He is. Take care of him, Lord.*

The next morning, Althea emerged from her bedroom, having come in late. She yawned and stretched.

"Have you set a date yet?" Diana asked.

"No, but soon we think. We decided we didn't want

anything big. We would rather spend our money on getting settled into our own apartment. Depends on Roger's transfer. The wedding may be the end of June we think." They talked and laughed until Diana spied the clock.

"Oh gosh, I've got to go." She hugged Althea. "If there's anything I can do—"

"You'll have to help me pick out a dress. And you're going to be my maid of honor, remember?"

"I'll love it. Just tell me what and when." Diana blew her a kiss as she went out the door.

Driving toward the office, Diana began to think about all the changes Althea's leaving would bring about. The apartment would be empty. Even Osgood wouldn't be there. She'd have to find another roommate, unless she could afford the rent on her own. She and Althea had been together for so long, it would be lonesome without her. *Even so, I'm so happy for her.*

She had much to catch up with in the office and spent most of the day organizing her work load. The week went by without incident, except Althea and Roger made their plans, or rather they were forced to do so. Roger was appointed to the Little Rock Office to report within a week. He would scout an apartment while Althea planned a small wedding and packed her things.

Nick called on Friday to say the log shipment was arranged and would be delivered the following week.

"I haven't made the trip to the mine. I just haven't had time," he said. "Dan is at the site, and it hasn't been touched."

"Well," Diana told him. "When I got back here,

Althea had to plan her wedding. Roger's going to Little Rock, and I'm going to help her. I may not be back to St. Elmo until July."

"I just learned Jack's development has gone through," Nick said. "When you come, I'll arrange for you to have an interview."

"You really think Jack would be interested?"

"Yes, I do. I'll put in a good word for you."

"Thanks, Nick. I will sure think about it. After Althea leaves, I'll have to find another roommate or another job."

"By the way," he said. "I will pray that you take Jack's job."

"Oh, ho. Been reading your Bible?" She laughed.

"Yep, God answers prayer." Diana laughed.

"Glad you found that out."

Althea gave her notice at the hospital, went shopping for a wedding dress, and made arrangements at church. Before Roger left, they got the license. The pace around the apartment picked up. Even Osgood knew something was happening when the packing started. Diana watched all this, knowing that with Althea gone, life would be different, and with Osgood gone, and furniture gone, the apartment would really be empty.

Before the end of June, Roger found an apartment. They planned their wedding for the last Saturday of the month. Althea was a radiant bride in white, and Roger was the typical groom. Diana was maid of honor, happy for the couple, but sad too. *But I'll have my home in St. Elmo. That is, if it gets built on time. And Lord, I'd like to have a kitty like Osgood. With good friends around like Angie and Nick, I'll be happy.*

So she contented herself as she watched movers take Althea's things the week after the wedding. When they were gone, she looked around the apartment. She still had her bedroom furniture, but the living room was bare except for Diana's cedar chest. The dinette set had belonged to Althea, so it was gone. Diana's two bar stools stood sentry at the counter. With all the excitement over, the bleakness in the apartment, and the July 4th weekend, Diana decided to clear out and go to St. Elmo. She hadn't been there since the fire. Nick had not mentioned getting up to the mine from Leadville. He had been very busy with Sutton. After making arrangements with Angie, she packed a small bag and headed out. It was time to see what her cabin looked like.

At eight o'clock in the evening, she arrived at Angie's. The mountain air smelled so good. The sun was gone, and though it was July, secluded within the mountain range, twilight did not last long. Angie was waiting for her. Opening the door, she hugged Diana.

"So good to see you. We thought you'd never get back."

"I was wondering that myself," Diana said, laughing.

"Come, sit. Have you had any supper?" Diana shook her head.

"Well, I've got some roast beef. I'll make you a sandwich."

The two women chatted about the wedding as Angie bustled about her kitchen. She set a big plate on the table, complete with sandwich, pickles, and potato salad, along with a tall glass of milk.

"Now tell me," she said. "Will you find another roommate or go it alone?"

"I don't know. I really haven't had much time to think about that." Diana bit into the sandwich. "Right now, I think I'll try to go it alone." She drank some milk and smiled, "I rather think I'll be spending my weekends here with you, that is, if you'll still have me."

"Of course, my dear. Consider this your home." Angie fixed herself a cup of coffee and sat opposite Diana. "It gets lonesome around here with just me, and I suppose you should see what's going on up at your site." She said.

"Have you heard anything? I need to call Nick."

"Only that your cabin is looking better every day."

"I hope you're right and nothing's happened to stop it." Diana finished her sandwich and placed a call to Nick. There was no answer.

In the morning on her way to the cabin, Diana decided to stop at Nick's. As she pulled in the drive, she noticed a large, handsome RV, conveniently parked beside some Aspens. *Nick's parents are here! With all the wedding business I'd forgotten they were coming.* Nick greeted her with a big bear hug.

"Boy, am I glad to see you," he said. "I was beginning to wonder if you'd ever get back. Come on in. I want you to meet my parents." Nick's father, Joseph Cureau, grinned and took her hand. He was a solid, broad-shouldered man, with a shock of gray hair topping his tanned, square-jawed face.

"So you're Diana," he said. "We've heard a lot about you. It's a real pleasure meeting you." Jerilyn Cureau bustled out of the kitchen. The small, handsome woman smiled broadly. "Diana! We're so glad to meet you. Nick's told us about you. Come, sit down, dear. Can I get you a cup of coffee? Have you had breakfast?"

"Um. Yes on both," Diana said, and asked about their trip. They responded, telling about their travels. The four adults laughed and chatted easily, and Jeri served coffee all around. Diana liked Nick's parents almost immediately. They were the picture of parents anyone would want. *I could love these two so easily. Nick is so blessed.*

Then Diana asked Nick, "What's happening in the meadow?"

"I was afraid you'd ask that. Actually the logs are up and chinked. The roof isn't on yet, but the windows and rooms are framed in. Of course the cement was poured right after you left last time."

"Well, that sounds pretty good. Why were you afraid I'd ask?" She frowned.

"Well, things have been missing from Dan's campsite; a flashlight, a lantern, and an ax. Someone is up there, and we don't think it's a bear."

"Did you ever get over to the mine?"

"No, I haven't. I've been so tied up." Nick hung his head and scratched his neck.

Joe broke in, "Why not go out there tomorrow, Nick.

Take Diana. Jeri and I can watch this place. We'll feed the livestock."

"Livestock?" Diana was surprised. "You mean you have your horses here?" She looked at Nick who smiled broadly. She got up and went into the lanai to look out the big window. A neatly painted fence enclosed a corral, and at the far end stood a handsome stable and tack room. Belle and Champ were at their feed box, swishing their tails.

"What a lovely sight," she said.

Nick joined her, "How about riding up to the mine with me tomorrow? We'll take a picnic. Come prepared to ride Belle. There's a horse trail around the other side of the mountain. We won't have to go all the way to Leadville."

"I'd love it. Meantime, can we go over to the cabin?"

"Sure. But you'll have to promise to go out to dinner with us tonight." He stood looking at her, his thumbs hooked in his jeans.

"I'm sold," she said, grinning. Back in the living room, Joe had settled down with his paper, and Jeri was clearing the coffee cups.

"Mom, Diana and I are going to run over to the site. You and Dad be okay here while we're gone?" Nick asked.

"Of course. I'll put these cups in the dishwasher, and there's things I need to do out in the RV. Looks like your Father has found the paper. You two go on." Then she hugged Diana. "It's so good to have you here," she said. Diana flushed with pleasure.

As they got into Nick's truck, Diana said, "I really like your parents, Nick. They are wonderful. It's so easy to love them."

"They are pretty great. I knew you'd like them. And they really like you too." He smiled. "I knew they would."

As they approached the meadow, Diana could see her cabin. The walls had risen, doors and windows were defined, and the logs were chinked. *What a picture this will be. Lord, I can't believe this.*

Inside, a mason was putting his skill into the stone fireplace. Several carpenters were preparing the huge support beams for the second floor. Diana looked around the shell of her home. The partitions were marked, the stairs defined, and the upper floor was still on the blueprints. She was thrilled with the progress. Maybe, just maybe, she would someday occupy this lovely spot.

"Let's go find Dan and see what's up in his department." They walked carefully over tools and outside toward Dan's trailer. They found him outside, cleaning his rifle.

"Have you needed that, Dan?" Nick asked as they approached.

"Up 'til now I haven't. But last night I heard a prowler walkin' around up by the cabin. Duke, here, chased him off." The German Shepherd wagged his tail at the mention of his name. "He's been a good dog. Doesn't bark during the day. He knows who's supposed to be here." Dan rubbed his coat. Diana bent to stroke the animal.

He's well trained, ma'am. Best watch dog I ever had," Dan said.

"I remember our walk when we saw that man at the turn of the road. He knew who was supposed to be here then too," she said.

"Did you find out who was prowling?" Nick said, a frown on his forehead.

"No, sir. He ran off. He must have parked his car up on the road. I heard him start the engine. Probably turned it off and coasted when he came. That's why we didn't hear him."

"Anything missing?"

"No, Duke didn't give him a chance."

"Well, keep up the good work, Dan. You too, Duke. Let me know if there's anything you need." Nick rubbed the dog's coat and nodded at Dan.

Later, sitting on the rock, watching the activity of the workmen, Nick scratched his head, "You know, if the construction keeps on like this, your cabin will be finished by September."

Diana sighed, "But I can't get away from an uneasy feeling, Nick. My mind tells me someone doesn't want me up here."

"I have all the bases covered, Ed Robins is still working his investigation, and whoever it is will tip his hand soon enough."

"Have you talked to him? Has that missing employee ever been found?"

"He came back to work. Said he had to make a trip back east. Something to do with family. Arson is still sus-

pected, but an arsonist is very hard to prove and convict."
They sat silently for a long time.

"Let's go see Jack at the Skyline Inn and have some
lunch," Nick said, jumping down off the rock. They
left and drove to the Inn. The sun was nearly overhead.
Entering the valley which lay at the foot of the Inn, they
came upon workmen with heavy equipment, moving
piles of earth.

"Nick, you didn't tell me. What's happening here?"

"The deal went through. Sutton, Danbury & Foster.
Only it's going to have a Swiss Village atmosphere
instead of an old mining town. The Skyline Inn has a
huge business in the winter with the ski crowd, and they
decided to use that theme but build up the summer trade
too. And the Inn will have more units back behind what's
there now." He parked the truck and came around to her
door. "I want you to talk to Jack. He's interested in your
skills."

They went inside and were seated. The waitress took
their order, and Nick asked if Jack was on hand.

"I'll tell him you're here," she said, smiling and turning toward the kitchen. Being early, the dining room was
almost deserted. "Next year this place will be jumping.
Jack will have triple the hotel units and another ski lift
is planned," Nick said. "The summer crowd will enjoy all
the shops and restaurants, same as the skiers, but there
will be a theme park open with rides. Craftsmen and art-
ists can set up shop. It has a lot of promise."

"And I can see you're excited about it," Diana laughed.
"It sounds wonderful."

"You'll be excited too when you talk to Jack." Lunch arrived, and the waitress indicated that Jack was in his office and wanted to see them when they finished eating.

Later they tapped on his door and entered when he answered. Pleasantries exchanged, Jack apologized for not opening the door. He was seated at his desk, which was littered with papers, envelopes, and unopened mail.

"I'm about buried under all this," he said, laughing. "I think I need help. I've got contracts to consider, we'll be franchising later, and that's not even talking about the construction. The word gets out and everyone wants to get in on the act."

"The town's buzzing over all this too," said Nick. "Any opposition we felt has suddenly melted. I think they've realized what a boom to the area this whole project will be."

"Diana," Jack leaned back in his chair and placed his hands behind his head. "I need someone to handle all this, make contacts for me, be my right arm. I think you have the skills I need. Would you be interested in submitting a resume?"

"You don't want to go through my company in Denver?"

"No, the position will be permanent. Even after the project is completed, there will be management needed. We'll have to have a computer network." Diana suddenly began to see where she might fit in.

Flushed and excited, she said, "I'm terribly interested.

The whole project sounds wonderful. And if you think I might be useful, I'd love to give you a resume."

"Before W. F. passed on, he told me about you. He said if this thing ever got off the ground, I should talk to you first. I'd known him for years, and I trust his judgment," Jack said.

"Tell you what I'm going to do," Nick cut in. "I'll leave you two for a while. I'm sure you have lots to discuss. I want to see what's happening out there with the big equipment, and I want to talk to the foreman."

He saluted as he left the room. Diana began with questions, and Jack answered, giving her an overview of what the position required. He brought out plans and renderings, explaining the history behind the project. Other personnel would be hired, because the job would entail more work than one person could accomplish. So management would become one of her duties.

For an hour they talked. Diana was more encouraged as time went on. She could feel herself drawn to Jack, to the freshness of the enterprise, and the idea of family entertainment. The added bonus would be living in St. Elmo. *It's a dream come true, if my cabin gets built without trouble. Lord, I trust you with all of this.*

She promised to send Jack a resume with a cover letter when Nick returned.

In the truck, Nick turned anxiously to Diana, "Well, what do you think?" She glowed.

"I love the idea. I would really be moving to St. Elmo too. I think working for Jack would be a wonderful experience, and I know I could do it. But I'm concerned about the cabin. It'd be my home," she said, with a far away look in her eyes and satisfaction in her voice.

"And we'll make sure it gets finished," Nick said.

They drove back to Nick's, and he took her out to the corral. The afternoon air was still and dry. The two horses immediately came for a treat, and Nick produced two small apples from a basket in the tack room. After treating them, Nick took her hand and led Diana around to the back of the stable away from the house.

"What? Where are we going?" Diana said.

"Just here," and he turned her around and looked at her, his eyes sparkling. "I want you to know, I found Jesus Christ while you were gone." She caught her breath.

"You did?" Her eyes popped open.

With his voice low, Nick stated his news evenly with confidence while he held her hands.

"John Chambers and I spent one evening together in his study. I was reading John and wanted to talk to him about it. He explained about The Word being Christ. He took me into other parts, including Genesis. I understood about Israel, God's chosen people. It was through them that He sent His Son, but they rejected Him. He is the second person of the trinity, a perfect human being, He is God. He gave Himself as a sacrifice on the cross for my sins, and He rose again. I've been forgiven, and I accepted Him, and I haven't been the same since."

As Nick talked, Diana's eyes grew wider and a grin began to spread across her face.

"Oh, Nick, I am thrilled for you. I've been praying for that. Thank you for sharing."

"I can't read enough in my Bible," he said. "I'm through Acts and Romans. I am amazed. It makes sense, like a light went on."

"I know." She grabbed his hands. "That's exactly what happened to me. It's like you were blind but now you see." She slid her arms around him and hugged him joyfully. Then she backed off, brushed herself a bit, and looked down.

"Uh, sorry I did that."

"I'm not sorry; you can do it any time you want." He resumed holding her.

"I am just so happy you belong now," she said. "You are a child of God. He loves you."

He smiled down at her. "I am more convinced than ever that W. F. and God planned all this. And I think it's going to get better and better."

Then she laughed and hugged him close again. "I like this."

"I do too, God is so good," he said, and they stood, his cheek against her hair. After a long moment, he said softly, "You are going to dinner, aren't you?"

Without looking at him she nodded, "If you say so."

"I say so." After dinner, driving back to Angie's, Diana glowed, remembering Nick's parents and the progress of her cabin. *And best of all, Nick's a real Christian. Thank you, Lord. Please protect my cabin. See that it's completed, please. I want Your will.*

• • •

"So do not fear, for I am with you; do not be dismayed, for I am your God. I will strengthen you and help you; I will uphold you with my righteous right hand," (Isaiah 41:10).

Twelve

"For I know the plans that I have for you, declares the Lord. Plans to prosper you and not to harm you, plans to give you hope and a future," (Jeremiah 29:11).

Diana had crawled out of bed, opened her bible, and sat in the chair by the window. Early-morning sun was just peeking through the window. As she was reading, she smoothed her hand over the silky pages, appreciating what God was telling her. The aroma of fresh-brewed coffee wafted up the stairs. *Thank you, Lord, for that promise: a future, even though my cabin has a shadow over it.*

She yawned, stretched, and decided to shower. Dressing in jeans, boots, and a long-sleeved plaid shirt, she brushed her hair and descended for breakfast.

"Good morning," Angie said. "You look ready for the back country."

"More so, I hope, than the last time," Diana said. "It's going to be a long day, I think."

"Sit down, dear. Breakfast is ready." Angie brought

eggs and bacon, toast, jam, and coffee, and the two enjoyed the meal together.

When Diana arrived at Nick's, he was saddling the horses. Jeri greeted her at the door. After a bit of small talk, she offered coffee and Diana declined.

"I've put together a lunch for you two," the older woman said. "I assume you'll be gone most of the day."

"That was very thoughtful of you, thank you. And while I think of it, please know how much I enjoyed being with you last night at dinner. It was lovely."

"We enjoyed it too, my dear. It's so good to see Nick happy again. Last time we were here, he was so down. You are just what he needs." Jeri smiled and squeezed Diana's hand. A moment of understanding passed between them.

Joe and Nick came through the back. Diana was greeted and hugged by the older man, who turned to his son and grinned, "You take good care of this little lady today."

"Don't worry, Dad, I intend to." He turned to Diana with a bow, removing his black stetson in a gallant sweep. "Your mount awaits, m'lady." Diana giggled.

"Well, in that case, I'd better go mount the mount! I just hope I haven't forgotten how."

"You're going to need a hat!" Jeri said and bustled off. Nick picked up the lunch as she came back with a buff, leather cowboy hat. "I'll bet this one will fit you." And she placed it on Diana's head. "There. How does it feel?"

"Good. Thank you."

"Now they match." Jeri laughed. "Besides, the sun will get awfully hot out there. You'll be glad you have it."

They waved as they rode out. Nick led through the grove of trees to the trail, taking them up over the ridge. When they stopped at the top, her cabin was just visible through the pines below. The air was crisp and still in the early morning. The smoke from Dan's campfire curled up through the trees.

"Dan's having bacon for breakfast, I can smell it." Diana sniffed. "I will never tire of seeing this vista," she said. "I remember the first time we stopped here. Like being on top of the world. So peaceful." They gazed around for a long moment, neither speaking.

"There's where our trail to the mine takes off," Nick said, pointing to the right around the ridge. "Instead of descending, we'll continue that way. It's rough-going in places. It takes us all the way around the mountain so we come in from the west. Eventually we'll cross the road from Leadville."

They followed the trail. The horses were eager to go, and Diana relaxed, allowing Belle to follow Champ. They climbed above the trees and continued over the trail that seemed invisible at times. The horses were sure-footed, and Diana gave Belle her rein. They threaded through some huge boulders, jutting from the mountainside, and here the trail leveled out into a grassy meadow, dotted with wildflowers. Tall pines reached toward the sky, and aspens, their silver-like leaves fluttering, clustered off to the side. They stopped at a small stream to water the horses and rest a bit. Dismounting, Diana welcomed the chance to stretch.

"This is a lovely place," she said.

"It's your land. Pretty secluded. Nobody gets back here much. Great place for a picnic." Nick found a flat rock and perched on it. Diana joined him. The horses edged off toward the grass.

"I can see some backpacking possibilities too. Good place to get away," Diana observed.

They sat on the rock for a long minute in silence, listening to the rustle of the wind in the aspens and the cry of a hawk circling overhead.

"I claimed a promise from my Bible this morning," Diana said. Nick turned to look at her.

"What is it?"

"I know the plans that I have for you, says the Lord, plans to prosper you and give you a future. It's from Jeremiah 29:11." He smiled and looked deeply into her blue eyes.

"God will see your home to completion." Nick bent down and gently kissed her. Then he glanced at his watch.

"We'd better get on with it."

"How much longer?" she asked.

"Probably an hour. We'll stop and eat first." Nick stood and pulled her up. "Are you okay for the next lap?" he asked.

"Yes, I think so." She brushed herself off. "I hope we don't find anything, and at the same time, I hope we do. If the mine is deserted, we've just had a nice day. If someone is there, we might have trouble. And that scares me."

"You let me worry about the trouble. I've come prepared."

"How?" she said, looking seriously at him.

"I've got a forty caliber automatic in my saddle bag."

"Oh, Nick, that scares me even more." She shuddered.

"Come on," he said. "We've got to get some answers. You're not supposed to worry." He led her over to the horses.

They rode on through the small meadow, then climbed up through the pines to open high country. Here the trail disappeared, and Nick reined in and waited for Diana to catch up. "See that peak up ahead," he pointed. "The mine is on the other side. We'll go around to the right and down. We'll come to the road. There's a stream over there, and we can stop and eat."

Later, tired and thirsty, they crossed the road and melted down into the trees beside the stream. Retrieving their lunch, Nick loosened cinch straps, and the horses went right to the water.

"The road looks like it's in real bad shape." Diana observed.

"It's not used anymore. Takes a four wheeler to get in there." Nick handed her a packet of sandwiches.

They ate, sitting on a blanket that Nick had tied on the back of her saddle. A bee buzzed by and a chipmunk skittered across a rock. He was looking for a handout. Diana tore a bit of bread and tossed it toward him. He grabbed it with two eager paws and stuffed it in his cheeks. He swished his tail in salute and was gone.

"He'll be back." Nick said. "You've spoiled him."

On finishing lunch, they gathered up their trash, stuffing it away with the blanket on the saddle. The few crumbs that were left were placed on the rock for the chipmunk. They climbed to the road, and the horses were eager to go. It provided a level surface, and they rode in silence for several miles. Nick reined his horse and Diana joined him.

"I think we'll ride down by the stream from here in," he said. "It's out of sight, and if there's anyone there, we can observe without being seen."

Diana followed Nick down the incline, through the trees, to the stream. They walked the horses, sometimes in the stream, then on the bank. An uneasy feeling gripped her. *Lord, please. Keep us from harm, and please see that Nick doesn't have to use that gun.*

They stopped, dismounted, and let the horses drink.

"We should walk from here." Nick said, looking at Diana. "You okay?" She nodded. "I've never been on this kind of a trip." She tried to smile. "I'm a little scared."

"I'll scout it out. You stay here with the horses." He reached for his saddlebag and extracted his gun.

"Nick, please be careful." Tucking the gun inside his shirt, he kissed her lightly. "I will. I'll be back in a while. Just stay here and relax."

She sat fidgeting in the shade on a large rock beside the stream. She tried to think about other things. The sun was overhead, and the day was warm. She focused on the history of this place, when the old prospector worked his mine. This was where he got his water and fish too, she supposed. And maybe he pitched his tent here. The peace of the place, and her thoughts didn't stem her anxiety. Expecting to hear a gunshot any minute, she finally heard him approaching.

He came through the trees and sat down beside her on the rock.

"Someone has been there all right. There's tire tracks, and inside, some tools and a couple of buckets of rock where they've been working. I picked up a piece. Think I'll have it assayed."

"If whoever is up here finds something valuable, I guess that would be good reason to not want me here," she said.

"Especially since you'll own the property. I think we'd better stick to the stream and be out of sight of the road 'til we have to cross it, just in case they return." He held up the rock from the mine. Tiny flecks glistened here and there in the jagged edges. "Could be they've found something," he said.

They mounted and rode carefully along the stream. At times they rode the horses through the water until they needed to pick up the back trail. Stopping at the spot where they had eaten earlier, Diana noticed the scraps were gone. As the horses drank from the stream, a dirty, green four-wheel drive Ford Explorer passed along the road toward the mine.

They crossed the road and went up through the trees toward the meadow. Diana's thoughts churned. *I wonder*

*what is in that rock. If it has something to do with the trouble,
the fire, and, Lord, what does it all mean for my cabin?*

She began to feel the muscle strain of the ride, and
realized she was aching from fatigue. When they stopped
to rest in the meadow, Nick helped her down.

"I know what you've been thinking and worrying
about," he said. "I'm going to get this sample checked
out, talk to Robbins and have him check on Bonar's car,
what kind it is and who else has a green Explorer, either
in Leadville or St. Elmo. Whoever's up there, they have
no business being there. That land belongs to Sutton until
your cabin is built. They are, at the least, trespassing." He
looked into her eyes. "So now we have something to go
on, okay?" He held her at arm's length, "Trust me?" She
smiled.

"I do. I will." And she hugged him closer.

By late afternoon, they could see Nick's home below
through the trees, and at five o'clock, they were stabling
the horses.

"You'll have to stay for supper," Nick said. "If I know
Mom, she'll insist on it. And they'll want to know what
we found."

Later, after all the conversation concerning the day,
Nick called Ed Robbins to report their findings, and
Diana phoned Angie. Nick agreed to meet with Ed in
the morning at the station, and Angie said she would
leave a light on for Diana. Jeri bustled about over dinner, and Joe followed Nick around discussing supposi-
tions and possibilities. Diana sank onto the sofa. She
was tired to the bone. And she felt every muscle. With

mixed thoughts of the day, she drifted off to sleep and was awakened an hour later when Nick brushed his hand against her cheek.

"Dinner's ready."

After they ate and the dishes were put away, Diana kissed Jeri and hugged Joe, thanking them for the evening. Nick walked her to the car, "I'll call you tomorrow after I see Ed and take that sample to the assay office. Will you be okay?"

She smiled, "After a hot soak in the tub, good as new." She turned the ignition as he brushed his hand softly against her cheek.

"Take care," he murmured.

Angie was still up and needed to hear the details. Then Diana escaped to the tub and bed. She slept almost immediately. It was ten o'clock in the morning before she stirred. When she did, she found muscles stiff and sore. Putting her robe on, Diana found some aspirin in the bathroom.

Early afternoon, Nick rang the doorbell. Angie answered.

"Hello, Angie, I brought you some daisies. Hope you like them." Nick held out a small bunch of white, African Daisies.

"I love daisies, come on in," she said, taking the flowers and going off to find a vase.

"Hello, Diana. I thought I'd stop by and tell you about what Ed's doing." She motioned for Nick to sit on the other end of the couch. "He agrees that whoever is up there has no business being there. He's checking on that vehicle we saw, talked to Leadville about that too. The assay will take a little more time. We're sending that off to Denver. I've been up to the site. Told Dan about what we found and he's alerted. Not much more we can do but wait." He paused, scratched his neck. "Oh yes, the second floor is in and the roof will be up this next week. It's coming along."

"And there isn't really anything I can do but just wait and trust, I guess, and pray."

"That's right, and get your resume off to Jack as soon as you can."

Coming back into the room with the vase of daisies, Angie said, "Oh yes. And give your notice and move in here until your cabin is finished. I would love the company."

"I will if Jack hires me."

Diana looked at these two people. *You mean so much to me. Your hospitality, your friendship, and, Nick, you want me here, and you're both putting yourselves out for me. I won't give up. I'll fight. I love you both.*

• • •

"Commit to the Lord whatever you do, and your plans will succeed," (Proverbs 16:3).

Thirteen

Leaving St. Elmo Tuesday morning after the holiday, Diana reached her office by 8:30 without stopping at the apartment. Greeting the receptionist, she collected her messages and went straight to her desk. By mid-morning, she had organized and prioritized her work so that she was able to spend her lunch hour updating her resume. The cafeteria produced a wonderful meatball sub to go, and she quietly slipped back to her desk, told her secretary that she didn't wish to be disturbed, shut the door, and proceeded with her resume. The CEO was away on vacation, as was a good third of the staff. Not much was happening. Within the hour she finished it, printed it, and placed it in an envelope along with a cover letter. *Lord, please honor this if it's your will, and I believe it is.*

She sealed it, stamped it, and placed it in the mail-out box. Then she looked around the office, took a big breath, and realized it was possible she would be giving her notice. This place used to be an anchor, a place to spend energy accomplishing something important. It no longer was. She wouldn't miss it. Nor would anyone here miss her. It was a large company. She had made friends, but they came and left just like Roger. *I hope Jack hires me.* Finishing her work by five, she headed toward the apartment, stopping for a hamburger at McDonald's.

Wednesday evening Nick phoned. He had heard from the assay office. There was gold in the sample, not a lot, but it was there.

"I thought that mine was worthless. At least that was the skinny all this time," he said. "I've wondered if W. F. knew about this. He probably didn't," he mused. "Anyway, he wouldn't have wanted any gold diggers in there. They would interfere with Sutton's objectives."

"What do we do now?" Diana asked. "Gold is a big motivation, and I suppose if the word gets out…"

"It won't get out. Those guys aren't telling anyone. You can be sure of that. Ed is checking on those vehicles. Bonar does drive a Ford Explorer. But Ed will have to catch him in the act of trespassing before he can make an arrest. That's pretty difficult country to stake out."

"Is there anything we can do now?" Diana asked.

"Nothing except build your cabin and get you in it. They won't be able to do too much there in the time it will take to finish. Besides, we don't really know if there's a connection between the mine and the trouble we've had."

Thursday passed, and on Friday she packed her bag and took it to work in order to leave from the office and be in St. Elmo by seven.

She cleared her desk, left word with the receptionist, and slipped out a bit early. It was good to get away from the city. The air smelled fresher, the sky seemed bluer, and the beauty of the passing landscape was invigorating. As she drove, she thought about the first time she came to St. Elmo, about W. F., and about her work at Sutton. Angie had said that things had changed since his death. Arbuckle was not W.F., and though the work and goals of the company remained the same, attitudes had changed. *It's amazing how one person at the top can set the tone of a whole company. And Carol, I've heard nothing about Carol for some time now. She used to buzz around Nick like a bee after honey. Obnoxious woman.*

When she pulled into Angie's drive, the front door was open and Angie was outside watering her garden.

"Hello. I was wondering if you'd be here this weekend."

"Angie, I'm sorry I didn't call."

"No need, dear. You aren't company, and this is your home for as long as you need it. I'm so glad you felt you could just come." She hugged Diana, and they walked to the house arm in arm.

Angie had a casserole in the oven, and with a bit more time, they enjoyed a meal together. Settling down for the evening, Diana mentioned Carol.

"I haven't heard one thing about her from Nick. It's been more than a month." She said.

"Don't know, except she might have gone back to New York. Actually it's been rather quiet here, and I haven't heard anything either. Come to think of it, she and Lloyd are usually high profile. Something must have happened." Both women were silent for a long moment. The telephone rang and Angie answered.

"It's Nick, Diana, for you."

"I thought you might be here," he said. "Stop by the house on your way out to the cabin. I have something I want to show you. Oh, and by the way, Jack got your resume. He told me he wants to see you. We can go out there tomorrow if you have no other plans."

Next morning after breakfast, Diana waved to Angie as she drove off. The sky was clear with a couple of wispy clouds, and the air smelled of pine. Driving up Nick's driveway, she parked and knocked on his office door.

Nick answered and pulled her inside. Closing the door, he hugged and kissed her.

"I'm so glad you're here," he said.

Diana backed off and looked around.

"What are you looking for?" he said.

"The last time I was in your office, Carol was here," she said, her eyes twinkling.

"Well, she's not here now. She knows better."

"Nick, can I ask you a question? Are we good enough friends to be honest with one another?"

"I sure hope so," he said. "Ask away."

"When I came here and Carol was here, I was sure she had spent the night. Is Carol one of the sins that Christ forgave?"

Nick drew close and looked at Diana soberly, his hands on her arms, "Yes, Diana. Christ forgave all that sin and what went before too." He paused. "And someday,

I will marry you if you'll have me. When I ask you, I want that to be a special day. I love you, Diana, and I want everything to be right for us in God's eyes." He took her in his arms and kissed her gently.

Her arms reached up and circled his neck. Finally he released her.

"Nick, thank you for that. I love you too." Her eyes were shining. "When you ask, I promise you'll get a positive answer. And God will honor it." She kissed him and rested in his arms.

Then he said quietly, "I have something for you." Drawing her over to an easel, he indicated the painting there. "Your cabin," he said. Her breath caught.

"Nick, it's beautiful. It looks like I could walk right up the steps. Thank you. I love it." She walked over and examined it closely. "You are so talented. It's perfect." She stood looking at the painting for a long time, moving close, then backing off. "It'll go over the fireplace." Then she kissed him tenderly.

While he held her close he said, "Darling, I'm planning to do something on my own to get to the answers about what's going on. I will be away. I can't say how long or where I'll be, and if anyone asks, I'm visiting family." He drew her away and looked into her eyes. "Okay?" She blinked.

"I guess this is where I really need to trust. I'm okay. I won't ask any questions. I love you, Nick." She kissed him again.

"Let's leave your painting here for now and go over

to the site." He smiled. "You'll be more impressed over there." Nick opened the door and led her to his truck.

The second floor was up and the roof was on. They walked through the structure, speaking to several workmen. Then Nick suggested they visit Dan, who was down by the stream fishing with Duke.

"Are they biting today?" Nick said as they approached.

"Aw, caught my supper, two in the creel," Dan said.

"Had any trouble since I last asked?" Nick said.

"Nothing stolen. A couple of prowlers, but Duke chased 'em off." Dan reeled in his line and secured his gear. "Come on back to the trailer and set a spell."

Walking back, Nick told him, "I'll not be around for a while, Dan. I can't say where I'll be or how long I'll be gone. In reality, I don't know. But if you don't see me, you'll know I'm away. I'll square it with Sutton."

"Don't you worry about everything here," Dan said. "Duke and I will keep watch. Any strangers around here will not be welcome."

"Thank you, Dan, and you too, Duke." Diana stooped to stroke the dog.

"Thanks, Dan. We can't stay. We have an appointment and lunch," Nick said. They took their leave and went toward Nick's truck.

"I won't ask for any details, Nick," Diana said. "Only, when will you take off?"

"And, darling, I won't tell you, only because I don't want anyone to know, so if someone would ask, you could only tell what you know. But know this, Diana, I will be back with more information than we have now." He opened the passenger door and kissed her. "And I will be back for you."

"Be careful, Nick."

"I will."

At the Skyline Inn they ordered lunch, asking the waitress to let Jack know. She returned with a message to come to the office. Jack was overjoyed to see them. He was still covered up with papers.

"Seems the last time I was here, your desk was just like this." Diana smiled as Jack welcomed them.

"Yes, it just keeps on. It won't go away. That's why I need you. Are you ready to come aboard? Your resume tells me you are just what I need." He came around his desk and took her hand. "Will you come work for me?"

"Yes, sir. I'll need to give my notice and move my things into storage. I could be here shortly after that."

"Nick, it's good to see you. Thanks for bringing her by."

Shaking his hand, Nick said, "You probably want to show Diana around. Mind if I see what's going on out with the workmen?"

"Not at all." Jack pulled up a chair while Nick left.

He made a salary offer, and she accepted. He agreed to pay for a moving company's services and gave her information on the nearest storage facility. Then he said, "I'd like you to see what we're planning."

For a time they rode in his golf cart around the buildings of the development. From time to time, they passed Nick, who waved as he talked to the workmen, who were all over the area like bees. Heavy equipment was still moving earth for future structures, and Diana could see the beginning of a gigantic project that would not be completed until next year.

Jack introduced her to his foreman, who showed her some blueprints. Then Jack suggested she see the ski lifts and the winter buildings. They rode through trees to a clearing, and on the far side was a large warming house, now closed. She could see the chairs from the lift station in the clearing, ascending up the mountain to another platform at the top.

"We have summer vacationers who want to see the countryside," Jack said. "So Jon's here to give rides to the top." Jack introduced the young fellow and asked if she'd like to ride to the top.

"This one's on the house." He grinned as they were strapped into the seat. Jack pointed to the different ski slopes as they ascended.

"This place is busy in the winter. People come from all over to ski these slopes. The snow is dry and perfect."

"It's beautiful up here now." She looked off to the higher vistas and then back down to the top of the Inn and the builders with their heavy equipment. They jumped off when the chair came to the platform of the first level.

"We run only this lift in the summertime. The next one goes higher up above timberline. That's where the professionals like to ski. We have a first-aid station here in the winter in case of accidents." He pointed to the glassed-in enclosure beside the platform. Jack pointed in a couple of directions, telling her about the area's history, and finally he suggested they should descend. Catching one of the chairs, they strapped themselves in and enjoyed the ride down. Nick was waiting for them.

"Did you like what you saw?"

"What a wonderful layout, Nick. Yes. I liked everything."

"And I'm going to like having her work for me," Jack said.

"Let me know when you can be here, Diana. I'll hold the fort."

They drove away with Diana reveling in her tour and telling Nick how much she was looking forward to her move.

"I'm glad you insisted that I send my resume. Jack will be a great boss to work for, and this project is so right. People will come here for recreation and fun. Families will be blessed too. And I will be blessed. God is good." She smiled up at him.

"And W.F. is up there smiling," Nick said.

• • •

"Blessed are all who fear the Lord, who walk in his ways. You will eat the fruit of your labor; blessings and prosperity will be yours," (Psalm 128:1–2).

$\mathcal{F}$ourteen

Returning to Denver, Diana gave her notice at work, contacted a moving company, and told her apartment manager. When all the dates for this were established, she wrote to Jack that she could be in St. Elmo to work by the middle of August. So much had to be done before that time. She had to finish a project at work involving a company in Denver, pack her things, say goodbye at church, and keep up with her cabin in St. Elmo. She was soon in a swirl of activities.

Her apartment was nearly bare. She decided one evening to visit a mall and find a couple of chairs to sit on. In one sports store she discovered folding director's chairs and purchased two with blue canvas backs and seats. Not having a television, she bought one in Macy's and came home thinking she would do well to keep up with the news at least. Angie called on Wednesday.

"Just wondered how everything's going, dear," she said.

"I've arranged my life but not done any packing. I bought a TV and a couple of folding chairs. I'll wait until I move for the big stuff," Diana said.

"Good girl. I'd come help you, but I figure I can be of more help on this end when you really move in."

"That sounds good. I don't know where I'd sleep you here. I won't be there next weekend; I think I should tend to business here," she said. On Thursday Nick called.

"Just wanted to know what you are doing. I'm lonesome."

"I am too, Nick. Right now I'm filling a big box with winter clothes. And there's more to do too. I've just scratched the surface. What are you doing?"

"I'm packing too. Leaving tomorrow. Everything's in control here. Ed's keeping a tight watch on Bonar, and Dan's at the site."

"Who's feeding your horses?" She asked.

"One of Ed's men offered to come over each day. He has horses of his own." He paused. "Honey, I'll miss you."

"Me too, you." She squeeked and swallowed a lump, she wouldn't see Nick and didn't know how long that would be.

He was quiet on the other end sensing her emotion. Thinking to change the subject to happier things, he said, "When you come you'll need to pick out your kitchen appliances at McKelvey's. They have a list of things you'll need to choose. And whatever you get is paid for. They have carpet and tiles, or maybe you'll want hardwood floors. Your choice. There are other things on the list.

Lots of decisions, love. Have a good time." He added. She recovered her voice.

"Sounds like fun. Nick, please take care of yourself. I'll be praying for you."

"Thanks, hon. Remember, the Lord goes with me."

The next two weeks she packed at night, did project work out of the office, and attended two farewell parties at church with friends. She heard from Roger and Althea, who were nicely settled, and she called to tell them about her move. Gradually she found herself living out of suitcases and boxes. Frozen dinners were stacked and then replaced in the freezer as time went on. Finally she could arrange to spend three remaining vacation days in St. Elmo before her move. Near the end of July she drove into Angie's driveway. It was early in the day, and the familiar sight was like home. Angie came out to welcome her with a hug.

"It's so good to see you. Let's bring your things in and have some lunch." Angie said.

"I'm so excited, Angie. After lunch will you go out to my cabin with me? I want to see what's been done. Nick told me I had to choose things off a list at McKelvey's. I'd better do that while I'm here. Would you help me?"

"I would love to. I haven't been out there for a month at least."

They drove to the meadow and parked beside five vehicles. The place was a beehive of activity. Workmen smiled and waved at them. Dan was there and Duke right behind him.

"Hello, Miss Laramore. Haven't seen you around for a spell. What do you think of your cabin now?"

"It's beautiful, Dan."

He was at the entrance and invited them inside. The chinked logs gleamed with a light patina, like the ambiance of a time when life was simpler. It smelled of new wood and lacquer.

"Has anything bad happened since I was here last? You know, anything stolen or smashed or…"

"No Ma'am. Duke's been on duty, and the place has been pretty quiet. The weather's been good." The two women climbed the stairs to find two bedrooms and a spacious bath off the master. The deck extended off the larger bedroom.

"I'm going to love this," Diana said.

"Did you see the bath off the hall here? It's lovely with an enclosed shower," Angie said. They spent time examining and comparing both bathrooms.

"I can see I'll need to choose a few things, like faucets. They're probably on that list I'm supposed to see," Diana said. Then they went out on the deck through the French doors of the larger bedroom. Stairs descended down to the ground. Angie came to stand beside Diana on the deck.

"Don't you love it. So peaceful here. I think the layout is perfect."

"I can put some flower pots up here and my two director's chairs," Diana said. "This is a wonderful place to sit and read."

"And, Diana, you'll have to order that braided rug you

admired, and start looking for the lovely things you want in this place."

"Oh, Angie, it will be such fun. I will love it here. Getting settled will be so exciting, and along with a new job, I'll be so busy. You'll have to help me."

"Anything I can do, I'm here," she said.

"Well, I think we'll stop at the appliance place when we leave here," Diana said. "I'll spend some time while I'm here choosing the immediate needs. When I leave this time, I won't be back until I move. Could you come out here several times and keep me tuned in on this place?"

"Oh, sure. But Nick will be around, won't he?"

"Nick's visiting family in Canada. I don't know when he'll be back."

The two descended the stairs, examined the kitchen, and wondered where everything would go. It was pretty bare with no cabinets installed. Some kitchen blueprints were on the floor, and they stooped to examine them. One of the men came through and introduced himself.

"I'll be finishing your kitchen, Miss Laramore. I'm Henry, and anything you want, I can do." He described the completed kitchen and where everything would be. "It will have all-natural, wood grain cabinets, unless you want something else."

"Oh no, let's keep it that way. I love it."

As they drove toward town, Diana said, "You know, Angie, it's not really a cabin. It's a home for year round. I should think of a proper name for it."

"Wait 'til it's finished and you're there, then you'll know."

At McKelvey's, Diana chose the kitchen appliances and looked over the list of fixtures. She decided on brass to complement the wood, chose white tile countertops, and decided on hardwood floors.

The next day after Angie departed to the library, Diana went back to town to look at furniture and kitchen items. She was strolling the streets, looking in windows and enjoying the morning, when Carol walked out of Leslie's Dress Emporium ahead of her. Not being able to avoid the redhead, Diana resolved to be civil.

"Hello, Carol. How are you?" She said, smiling.

"Well, Diana. How fortunate meeting you without Nick around. I have wanted to warn you." She leaned toward Diana with a disturbed look on her face.

"Warn me? What about?"

"Nick. You see, I've known him for a long time, and we have an understanding. He's not going to allow you to live in your cabin. Don't be fooled by anything he says. He's only leading you on because of the will." Carol gave her a threatening look. She did not take her eyes off Diana.

"I find that hard to believe," Diana said evenly, not blinking but standing her ground.

"It's true." Carol advanced closer. And in a low tone, "You would do well to leave St. Elmo now before disaster strikes. I'm only concerned about you."

"And what are *your* plans for Nick, dear?" Diana said.

Taken aback, Carol, stumbling, said, "Why—what do you mean?"

"You just said you have an understanding."

"Oh… well, we'll be married in the Spring." Carol backed off and flippantly walked off down the street.

Diana could hardly keep from laughing. *Custer's Last Stand. Lord, you know I don't believe a word of that. Just guard Nick, give him wisdom, and bring him back safely. As for Carol, I think I need to pray for her, and, Lord, fence me round about.* She finished her shopping, selecting a table and six chairs, a sofa and matching love seat, and a master bedroom suite, mattress, and springs. Each item was ordered and would wait for a delivery date.

When she got back to Angie's at the end of the day, she told her friend about Carol's warning.

"You can't be serious," Angie said. "I can't believe any of that. How did you feel?"

"I had a hard time keeping a straight face. I asked her what her plans for Nick were, and she wasn't ready for that. I reminded her that she said they have an understanding."

"What did she say then?"

"She said they'd be married in the Spring and tripped off down the sidewalk."

"I think she lives in a rosy glow of her own making," Angie said.

"You know, Angie, Nick accepted Christ some time ago. I see the change. He told me the last time I saw him that he wanted to ask me to marry him, but when he does, he wants it to be the right time. There's no way that I believe Carol."

"Good girl. I'm glad to know about his intentions. Are you?"

"Oh, yes. I believe Nick, and I don't want to doubt him." *So if I believe him, I'll go right ahead with plans for my home.*

"I have tomorrow before I have to get back, so I think I'll go shopping for linens and dishes, pots and pans, and silverware. That should be fun. I know where to go now since I've done some window-shopping," Diana said.

"Good. There's plenty of room to store anything you get here in the house," Angie said.

The next day, Diana left mid-morning for town, with a list of her own making. She had a wonderful time choosing everything to set up housekeeping. She and Angie arranged to meet at The Hub for lunch. The waitress seated them at a table by the window.

"Well, tell me what you bought," Angie said after the waitress left with their order.

"Hmmm. Silverware, eight place settings of stainless, a simple design, not too ornate, dishes, a Franciscan pattern with service for eight, bed linens and a rose comforter set for the bed, some placemats. I need to find glasses and pots and pans. Eventually I'll need some of your famous recipes," Angie said.

"Sounds like you've made real progress." The waitress brought their cheeseburgers and fries.

"When I finish early this afternoon," Diana said. "I'll go back to Denver this evening. I'll have about twelve days until moving day, and I've told Jack I would start working on the fifteenth."

"Do you have much more to do in the apartment?"

"Most everything is packed, except a few boxes. The apartment needs a good cleaning."

"Why not hire that done for after you leave," Angie said.

"Not a bad idea."

Driving out of St. Elmo, she set her mind on the gritty business of moving. *Lord, please go before me, show me the pieces to pick up, and give me whatever I'll need, and be with Nick. Bring him home safely.*

• • •

"But encourage one another daily, as long as it is called Today, so that none of you may be hardened by sin's deceitfulness," (Hebrews 3:13).

*f*ifteen

The apartment was a bleak place to be with little furniture, a kitchen with nothing except a spoon, a dish, some paper cups, and boxes, boxes, boxes. Diana wondered often if she would need the things in those boxes. She also had the urge at times to light a match to the whole thing. *Oh, for a simpler life, Lord. Everything has meant a decision to keep or throw away. I'm tired and my head hurts.*

She spent a week winding up the project at work. The employees had a party for her the last day. Betty, one of the secretaries, gave Diana the number of a cleaning agency, and the office presented her with bon voyage balloons. When she got home, she collapsed in one director's chair and placed her feet up on the other. The balloons sat atop her TV, which was placed on her cedar chest. She looked around and spied the phone.

"Nick, I wish you'd call. It's been three weeks, and I miss you." She sat and stared at the thing, willing it to ring. It didn't. Then a little voice in her head said, *Suppose Carol was right?*

"No, I won't go there," she said out loud. But as she turned her TV on for the news and warmed her TV dinner in the micro, the thought nagged.

The next morning she called the cleaning agency who agreed to come in after she left. Then she arranged for the cleaning with the apartment manager, who made a note of the date. With five days to go until movers were due, she finished the rest of her packing, sorting what she would need until her cabin was completed, and what would go into storage. In between her goings and comings, she passed the phone and willed it to ring. It did ring several times with Angie on the other end.

"Hello, sweetie, how are you doing?"

"Oh, okay."

"You sound discouraged."

"I am. I just wish Nick would call. I know I'm not supposed to worry, but it's been a month. Have you been out to the cabin?"

"Just came from there. It's beautiful. The windows are in and the hardwood floors are being laid. Did you order that rug?"

"Oops, not yet. I'll do that tonight."

On moving day, Diana loaded her car first thing and then went back inside to wait. *Nick, please call. I wish I could know what you're doing. Have you forgotten me? No, I can't think that, yet I wonder. Carol, what kind of a hold does she have? What does she know? Nick, please call.*

Finally the movers came. Everything disappeared into

the truck, and by afternoon, Diana was picking up trash, stuffing the bin, and letting herself out of the apartment. Keys were left at the office, and she was on her way to St. Elmo. She would soon go to work for Jack. *Maybe Nick is back in St. Elmo…*

Angie's hospitality was so refreshing and so alive. It was good to be back, good to smell the pines, and good to see Angie's flowers nodding in her garden. It was so different from the concrete of the city and the bleakness of the apartment.

"Everything okay? I'll bet you're tired," Angie said.

"Yes, I am."

"Well, let's have some supper."

Diana took her bags upstairs while Angie set the table. Truly she had spent more time in the warmth of this home than in her apartment in Denver, even when Althea was there. When they moved to the living room to watch a movie, while Angie's knitting needles clicked away, and Diana's bare toes snuggled under the couch cushion, it was like a scene replayed. She looked hard at the opposite space, remembering how Nick asked her what made her different from other women, and how she told him about her conversion. Then she remembered the two of them back of his stables and his telling about accepting Christ and the joy he had and how she hugged him. *Surely the Lord is protecting him. Christ said, "I will never leave you or forsake you." I must trust, whatever he's doing must take a long time.* She glanced at the phone, then over at Angie.

"Thinking about Nick?" Angie wondered.

"Yes, I can't help remembering what Carol said."

"Dig a hole and put all that in it. Nick is a man of his word. And he's got God's Spirit with him," Angie said. "Besides, whatever he's doing, he's doing it for you."

"You mean you figured out that he's not visiting family?"

"Yes, one can only visit family so long. My mother used to say, 'Fish and visitors smell in three days.' I suspected some days ago, when he didn't come back, that he was on a mission of some sort. I think he knew something about that mine on your property that he had to find out about."

"You are probably right, Angie. I'll try not to doubt Nick anymore."

"Honey, doubting is the road our humanity always takes. It's the great deceiver, and he sits on our shoulder, and he wants to break our faith. Tell him to leave. You belong to Jesus."

"Thanks, Angie. I needed to hear that. I'll just keep praying for Nick, and I won't let it bother me if I don't hear from him," Diana said emphatically.

"Those may be famous last words. Remember, God won't be angry if you keep going to him when you doubt. He forgives and picks us right up again."

Diana went to work for Jack in Mid August and was immediately captivated by the enormity of the project. Designing the system to control all the facets was a challenge. She was set up in her own office next to Jack, and soon became involved in the swirl of things that went on with the management of the operation. While at work she had little time to think about Nick. But after work she stopped by the meadow to see the progress of her home. Several times she asked Dan if Nick had been around. The answer was always no. She determined not to ask any more. *It only makes me want to doubt, to not believe. Nick said, "I'll come back for you." I believe he will come back. I must believe that. There's a greater good beyond me that he needs to come back for, for the meadow, for whatever God wants in that meadow. Lord, bring Nick back safely.*

• • •

"The Lord knows how to rescue godly men from trials and to hold the unrighteous for the day of judgment, while continuing their punishment," (2 Peter 2:9).

$\mathcal{S}$ixteen

September with Labor Day came, and the workmen announced that the finishing touches to her home were nearly complete. She could move in the second week of the month. As the work was completed, Diana called Jonathan Somes to determine how she could take possession. After a visit to his office to get the keys, she arranged for the movers and requested furniture delivery. On that day, she worked around boxes, directing the men with their deliveries and placing the items in appropriate rooms. She hoped she could remember what was packed in which box, since she'd neglected to label them.

Mid-morning Dan ambled over with Duke at his heels.

"Miss Laramore, I've packed up my trailer. It's been real quiet here for some time. Nick said he wouldn't need me to stay once you moved in. I just wondered if there's anything I can do for you before I leave?" Diana came down the steps to stroke the animal as she talked with Dan.

"I'm going to miss having you both here. I guess we never did find out who was behind all the trouble we had."

"No, ma'am. Probably just the ordinary summer pranks of some school boys. You know how they are."

"I suppose so." She paused thoughtfully. "Well, Dan, thank you for everything. And you too, Duke." She knelt to hug the animal while his wet tongue returned her affection. "I hope you two won't be strangers, now," She said.

"If you need anything, ma'am, just let me know." She watched Dan walk to his truck and trailer, Duke at his side. It was certainly the end of a chapter. They had been up here since May.

Nick hadn't come back, and she suddenly felt very alone. The meadow lay before her, surrounded by stately pines that marched up the heights. A breeze whispered through them and the sun glinted on the meandering ribbon of water where Nick fished that first day. The scene was pure peace, yet she felt uneasy. Shaking herself, she turned to the task at hand.

There were boxes to empty and cupboards to fill, a bed to make, and clothes to put away. There was so much to do, so she began to put her mind to it. Angie drove in after work to spend a few hours helping Diana get settled. Her cheerful hello echoed into the kitchen where Diana was lining cabinets with shelf paper.

"You're just in time to be put to work," Diana said.

"Not until you and I have a bite. I've been to McDonalds." Angie came in laden with sacks of French fries, hamburgers, and milkshakes.

They cleared space on the new table and spread the food. Angie admired everything new while Diana washed up. As they sat down to eat, Angie mentioned that she'd noticed Dan was not out there.

"Does that bother you?" She said.

"It did a little when he left, but I have to get used to the idea of living alone here. This place is perfectly safe and nothing has happened out here for at least a month."

"Would you like me to spend the night?"

"Heavens no. I'll be fine. I'll probably sleep like a log, I'll be so tired. Besides if I'm here in the morning I can get going early. There's so much to do."

They finished eating, and Angie offered to put linens on Diana's bed.

"So you can just fall into it," she said. Both women opened boxes until they found the necessary sheets and blankets. Angie climbed the stairs to the bedroom, and Diana resumed her work in the kitchen. Outside, twilight yielded to darkness, while the meadow waited for the moon to edge over the mountain. Inside, the time passed while busy hands found lots to do. About 8:30, Angie left for home, and Diana had a moment of uneasiness as she looked out on the blackness after the car lights disappeared.

The bubbling sound of water tumbling over rocks carried on the night air, and a crisp, September chill encouraged her to close and lock her door. Bone tired, she turned out lights and climbed the stairs. There would be time tomorrow to do the rest.

Knowing that she could not sleep, at least not just yet, she put on her jacket, turned off the bedroom light, and stepped out onto the deck. The night air was crisp with a myriad of stars overhead. The moon was now rising in the sky. Only the sound of water splashing over rocks in the stream below accompanied her thoughts. She sat on the top step and leaned against the log wall. *It's lovely, even at night. W. F. knew just what I needed. I wish Nick were here.*

A feeling of contentment flooded her and she sighed deeply. As her eyes adjusted to the dark, she could see the clearing. Beyond stretched the meadow with the pine-clad mountains, faintly outlined against the sky. A movement near the corner of the house caught her eye. Then the crunch of loose dirt riveted her gaze to the spot. A dark figure moved stealthily around the corner. She watched as it rounded the steps and disappeared under the deck. *I wonder if Dan forgot something?* Standing and descending the steps quietly, she peered into the darkness.

"Did you forget something?" She said.

Suddenly, the unfamiliar shape of a man loomed in front of her. She felt him grab her wrist and swing her around until she was in his grip with his hand covering her mouth.

"No, lady. And don't scream." His voice was low and menacing. She suddenly felt anger surging up through her body, and adrenaline shot through her like rock salt from a cannon. *He's going to hurt me!*

She bit his hand and jabbed her elbow into his stomach, breaking free from his grasp. Then he backhanded her, knocking her to the ground.

"Who are you? What do you want? You have no right here. This is my place," she shouted, holding her painful jaw. He pulled a small package from his jacket, held it, and struck his lighter.

"It's all right, lady, it's gonna be over soon," he said. In the brief glow, she saw a bundle of dynamite with a fuse hanging from it. *He's going to blow it up!*

Furiously she lunged at him, knocking him to the ground before he could light the fuse. The lethal bundle went skittering off in the dirt. Scrambling to get hold of it, she tore her jacket and got a mouthful of dirt as they fought to get to the dynamite.

Reaching it first, she grabbed it and looked to see where her attacker was. She saw a shiny object in his hand and she tried to move away. Just as he grabbed her, a shot rang out. He let go and staggered backwards. Diana collapsed in the dirt. *I've been shot!* Then she fainted. Next thing she knew, Nick was bending over her frantically rubbing her hands.

"Diana, wake up, wake up."

"I must be bleeding. I think he shot me," she said weakly, looking down to find the wound.

"No, he didn't shoot you. We shot him," Nick said. "He had a knife. He was going to cut you."

"Oh."

"Ed's here with two of his men. They've hand cuffed him, and they have the dynamite. You'll be safe now." Tears welled up behind her eyes.

"Nick, he was going to blow up my house and probably kill me too."

"I know, dear. But he can't hurt you now." Nick said as he gently urged her to stand. "It's okay now. It's all over." Ed Robbins left his men and came over to Diana. She heard his kind voice.

"Are you all right, Miss Laramore?"

With tears streaming down her cheeks, she nodded, "I think so."

"We've got our man," he said. "My officers have him cuffed, and they're taking him in. You'll be safe now." He patted her shoulder and turned to Nick. "We'll need you both at the station in the morning to press charges."

"We'll both be there, and thanks for everything, Ed," Nick said. The sheriff tipped his hat, and the men, one between them in hand cuffs, walked toward the road, their flashlights casting weird lights in the darkness.

Diana leaned into Nick and being unable to control the tears, she sobbed into his chest.

"It's okay, baby. Just let it all out." He held her close, then slowly led her up the stairs into the bedroom. Placing her on the bed, he switched on the lamp. He found some tissues and a glass of water with a couple of aspirins. After her tears were dried and most of the dirt washed off, she felt better.

"I must be a sight," she said. "There's dirt in my hair, and I'm all red and puffy."

"A sight for sore eyes," he said, laughing. "Hey, scoot over and let me sit down on the bed."

As she moved over and Nick sat down and kicked off his shoes, Diana said, "Nick, who was that man? Was that Bonar? Tell me what happened."

"I guess I'd better start at the beginning," he said, rubbing his neck and stretching his legs on the bed. "I flew to Denver. I decided to get a complete breakdown on the sample we got from the mine. I found out it had a big percentage of molybdenum." He turned to look at Diana. "That's a hard, metallic element. It's used in dyes and fertilizers and enamels. Those industries pay good money." He leaned back, placing both hands behind his head and sighed. "That means heavy equipment, and it's a big operation. It's something W. F. always opposed. It would undermine Sutton's conservation principles."

Then he sat up. Putting both legs on the floor, he turned to face Diana and brought one knee up on the bed. "I got suspicious and checked with a couple of big mining suppliers. I found out that Lloyd had ordered mining equipment under his own name. I figured then that he was behind all the trouble we've had this summer. So, I did a little more scratching and discovered, with Ed's help, that Bonar was connected with Lloyd. He's an explosives expert that Lloyd hired to investigate the mine, undercover of course. That's why he was employed at the mill." He paused and looked at her. "Are you okay?"

"I think so. Did he start the fire at the mill?"

"Yes. And he's the one we saw going to the mine."

"He might have killed me tonight." She covered her mouth with her hand. "How did you know?"

"We figured he wouldn't try anything as long as Dan and Duke were here. Duke would have torn him apart. But when you moved in and they left, well, we planned a stakeout, and sure enough."

"I'm numb."

"I couldn't tell anyone what I'd discovered. I just had to leave you alone as well as everyone else. I was afraid someone would tip my hand. When I left my family in Canada, and all the pieces came together, I went to the board in New York. I've also spent time with our big stockholders. Lloyd was defying company policy, doing it under his own name, and on land that was becoming yours."

"What's happened to Lloyd?"

"Nothing so far. We had to let this plan run its course to get evidence. Bonar is the evidence, and Ed will be paying Lloyd a visit, maybe even tonight. He'll go to jail along with Bonar." She smiled at Nick.

"God has been good. I've prayed for you, and I must admit there were times when I wondered if you would come back. I have missed you so." Then she looked at her hands. "I saw Carol downtown one day. She told me you really weren't going to let me move in. She said she had to warn me. It was tempting to believe her when you didn't come back," she said.

"But I said I would come for you."

"I know, and that's what I trusted." Then she smiled, looking at him out of the corner of her eye. "Carol also said that you and she had an understanding. I asked her what that meant. She said you and she were planning to marry in the Spring." Nick gasped.

"That little she-devil! She's an accomplice, you know. She's going to jail right along with Lloyd." Then he looked around the bedroom, scratched his head, and turned towards Diana.

"I want you to use your imagination. We're sitting at a table in a fancy restaurant. We're the only ones here. I've reserved the night just for us. Over there an orchestra is playing softly. You are lovely in a soft, blue dress, and I'm in a tux." Then Nick got down on his knees beside the bed. He reached in his jacket pocket and pulled out a small, velvet box. Handing it to Diana, he said, "I love you, darling. I've loved you from the beginning. Will you marry me?"

Tears in her eyes, she said, "Oh yes, Nick. I'll marry you. I love you. Oh how I love you." She moved to hug him as if never to let him go. He pulled her up and they clung together in the joy of the moment.

Releasing her, he said, "Well, open the box." She lifted the lid to see the sparkle of a large, blue-white diamond solitaire set in a classic platinum band.

"It's beautiful. It takes my breath away." He removed it from its haven and slipped it on her finger.

"Now will you set the date? I won't wait long," he said. She looked at the ring.

"Well, I have to get my house in order." She waved her hand in the direction of the boxes littering the room.

"What makes you think I'll let you live here?" He said with a grin.

"Oh Nick, I've come this far. I have to live here. It's my little house, my home." Diana pouted, sticking out her bottom lip. Nick raised her chin with his forefinger, searching her face.

"Our first argument. I know. How about if you get settled in here, plan the wedding, and when we're married we can live in both places. This will be our retreat, and we'll be together wherever we are, here or there. Okay?"

"Okay." She kissed him and he wrapped her in the warmth of his embrace. They stood in the circle of their love and commitment for a long moment. Then she said, "God is so good, Nick. He's answered all my prayers."

"Mine too," he murmured into her hair. Backing off, she looked around.

"The band's gone home, and they are closing up the restaurant. You'd better take me home, darling," she said.

"Good idea, before we get carried away," he said

They were married at Thanksgiving, in the church with all their friends and Nick's family attending. The bride was lovely in white satin, the groom handsome in a tux. They spent their honeymoon in the cabin that brought them together. Outside, the moon winked in the dark sky over the meadow. The wind sighed, and not far away, one could hear an owl hoot, if one were listening.

TO JOHN